Dedicated To:

Kim Clement
and
Martin Stuart.

Kim passionately lived for the Spirit. Without his example, I could not create these stories.

And for Martin's genius and inspiration, thank you for always believing in me.

These two men fathered my spirit and soul, and I am indebted to them both.

Legends of the Wind: Volume 1 with Jurri Schenck

www.loversdreamersandme.com
www.legendsofthewind.com

Cover art by Alisha Schenck www.alishasimaginarium.com

Published by Seraph Creative in 2021
United States / United Kingdom / South Africa / Australia www.seraphcreative.org

Typesetting & Layout by Feline www.felinegraphics.com

Printed in USA, UK and RSA, 2021

ISBN 978-0-6486986-2-3

VOL I

LEGENDs OF THE WIND

with Jurri Schenck

Published by Seraph Creative

ACKNOWLEDGMENTS

First and foremost, I want to thank my beautiful wife Alisha Schenck for suggesting how to make Legends of the Wind successful. Her vision, savviness, understanding, and wisdom are invaluable. Not only that, her perseverance and desire to help encourage and empower people are amazing. I am indebted to her for everything. Our shared journey has been full of big ups and downs, and yet she has been a rock for me. Thank you, Alisha. You are a great wife, mother, artist, and business leader.

I also want to thank Chris Blackeby for his friendship and wisdom in inspiring us to become a true son. His publishing company Seraph Creative has been amazing in getting us launched with these books.

Additionally, Linda Lurie has been incredible in her laying out and editing the books. Her wonderful, kind spirit has been a dream to work with.

Thank you to Pastor Linda and the original children of Living Faith Christian Church for allowing me to write for you and for blessing me with your precious lives. Serving with you my stories helped me to find my voice, Fathering through Film.

Thank you to Shawn Bolz for his foundational leadership during my time at Expression 58. Some of my greatest friends were met there. Shawn's celebration of hearing God's voice and the arts was incredible.

Thank you to Joanne Tan for her friendship and for suggesting to take all our wonderful, deep conversations and make them accessible through the podcast. Combining the stories with thinking mythically and helping inspire and encourage the audience has been amazing.

Thank you to Jim Ballinger, Eduardo Gutierrez, Linda Lurie, and Cindy Glasson for your editing and proofreading the text.

INTRODUCTION

There is power in storytelling, but there is even greater power when you can find yourself in your own story. This is the primary focus of Legends of the Wind. Original, unique, mythical, and magical stories let you discover your identity and destiny. Everyone is looking for their own story. Every soul, no matter where they are from, in time or history, seeks the same certain things: Who am I? Am I loved? What is my purpose? Where did I come from? What is my future?

Now, what if you could go to a magical library that resides in the realm of the imagination and find a book written about you? What if there were chapters of stories that were written about you? They don't have to be literal, they can be in any genre and style — this is the realm of the imagination. Wouldn't you want to read the stories written about you? What if these stories reveal your true identity and bring healing to you? What if they reveal your purpose and future? These tales have existed beyond time and live in eternity. The problem is having access. But now that is no longer an issue, and we see it demonstrated in the stories of Legends of the Wind.

Jurri Schenck was a recent graduate from USC's Cinematic Arts Production Program, and he ended up volunteering at Living Faith Christian Church in Northridge, California, in December 2007. He worked with teacher Pastor Linda and her elementary students ages 6-10. Jurri wanted to inspire the kids and help them understand their identities and destinies. He got an idea: "What if I place the kids in their own myths, fairy tales, and adventures? What if I wrote them in their own stories?"

It turned out to be a tremendous hit! The kids loved seeing themselves in their stories and would even play and act them out while Jurri read to the class. The pastors and parents freaked out. They said, "We have never seen this done before." Jurri tapped into the kids' lives without knowing them in detail. Jurri discovered in his unique work an authentic voice and called it "Fathering Through Film". He could see that the stories bestowed identity and created a spirit of adoption for the hearts of the children.

After each reading, Jurri and Linda would ask the kids thoughtful questions to see if they could find the hidden treasures written in their story. Jurri learned identity and destiny are best caught by revelation, not taught directly. So in the stories, he would create images that represented ideas, and then through discussion and questions, the kids would discover those hidden meanings. After six months of this storytelling modeling, the kids no longer needed Jurri or Linda's prompts. They learned to do it themselves! This is what we call "Thinking Mythically."

What does it mean to think mythically? It starts with the story and looking for deeper meanings in them. It also means to look at your own life and see who you are in your own story. Where am I on my hero's journey? Who am I and what do I need to overcome? What are my heart's desires and where are they leading me? How can a story show me my true identity and my future? How can these stories bring healing to my heart? How can storytelling enlighten my eyes and let me see the truth and no longer believe the lies? How can these fairytales and fables show me life?

Jurri not only wrote for children, but he made connections with people at another church called Expression 58, led by Shawn Bolz. Those stories impacted their lives. At Expression 58 Jurri met his wife Alisha Choi, an illustrator and concept artist with a degree from ArtCenter College of Design in Pasadena. Jurri's stories continually moved Alisha's heart. Together they make an unparalleled creative team with her images and his storytelling.

Legends of the Wind's books are short stories written about actual people. Jurri never interviewed or researched anyone he wrote about. And yet somehow, with his special gift, he could tap into the specifics of the people. Some may call it psychic or prophetic or intuition. We should also take special note that no one has done something like this before. A psychic might give a reading that speaks of the past and the future. A prophet might tell someone in a direct language in their words, but as far as we know, no one has done this type of work with an actual person and tell them their story. Because the story's writing in a way unlocks the reader's own personal story, there can be no wrong interpretation.

Every person who has received a story has had their hearts touched. Their Legend speaks to them for the rest of their lives. The Legends are powerful as many people have cried or jumped for joy when receiving one. The stories are unique because each person is different. Yet, all of us can benefit from their story. There is a universal appeal to these tales.

There are over 65 stories already written with more volumes in the works. Legends of the Wind is a continuing exploration of people discovering their stories.

Everyone has a story. What story are you in? Would you like to find out? Do you want Jurri to help you find your adventure of a lifetime? Go to www.legendsofthewind.com to discover more. You can sign up for our newsletter for updates or promotions. You can also see some podcast episodes of Jurri and a guest listening to a story and modeling what it means to think mythically. Come and discover your own tale in Legends of the Wind.

CONTENTS

THE FIRE BEAR

Once in the dark forest, high in the mountains, there was a young cub, a grizzly bear cub. He was a bit big for his age, and sometimes when he walked he would growl and shiver and cry out into the night—for he was hungry.

Out by the stream, in the dawning of the day, he would try to snatch fish out of the waters. Over and over and over he would swipe his paw to catch a tasty morsel. But he would find none. Again he cried out — for he was hungry.

During a long hot day, he walked up and down the side of the forest and by the banks of the stream of waters. He was groaning, for he was angry. And on top of that, the badger, and the weasel, and the raccoon came off at a distance and laughed at the grizzly bear cub.

"HA! HA! HA!" they cried out. "It looks like the grizzly bear is hungry. Why don't you catch some fish, bear?" They fell backwards, laughing. They laughed so hard they couldn't breathe because their sides hurt.

Inside this bear, this cub, this young, mighty bear of the dark forest, high in the mountains, was fire and anger. He shouted back to the badger, the weasel, and the raccoon. "Shut up! You know I'm hungry! Why don't you pick on someone your own size?" The bear didn't realize that he was larger than the animals who mocked him.

But the badger and the weasel and the raccoon laughed even more. "He can't catch a fish! NA NA NA NA NA!" And they blew raspberry noises at him.

Well, the bear cub ran off far away, hurting, and found himself deeper in the dark forest.

Still hungry, he dug deep into the rich, black earth, searching for food. He found roots and nuts and branches: small onions and various underground grubs. These he ate, and they satisfied his stomach.

But inside his heart was fire and anger. He didn't know what to do with them. The fire inside of him was burning. Every time he spoke or growled about the fire, it would burn hot in his inner being and — it was good — as if true life were coming out of him. The fire was great, and it was his passions and his desire. And every time he growled about the fire, it reminded him of his future.

"What is this future and fire?" he wondered. "Where is this fire taking me? What does it speak of? How can I be of good use to it?"

For even though it was fire, it was good. Yet there was the anger, and that was a mystery to him. What can he do about it?

The grizzly bear cub again wandered in the forest and night came. Now, you might ask, where is the cub's family? Where have they been all this time?

Well, as this story goes, his mother bear and father bear were with him in another part of the forest hunting for more fish. And this young cub stood out on a log that stretched out over the river that was rushing fast.

He thought to himself, "This water rushes; it will bring me many fish, nice and quick!"

But his mother bear and father bear warned him not to get into danger. Fast times and fast motions always lead to something harmful.

The young cub didn't listen. He only heard his stomach.

So, off he went and stretched himself on the log, peering into the rapids. He saw many fish blazing by. "Oh!" he cried. "Now I will have a great meal."

And then, with a great sweep of his arm, he went to snatch a fish out of the water. But, then with a SNAP! the log he was on broke into two pieces and rolled down and the bear cub fell into the raging rapids.

For some time, the bear cub gasped and squirmed about, reaching for the air. But it was too late. The water's flow took him from his family, and now he was away from them. Night after night he would cry out, hoping against hope he would see them again.

Well, that was what happened in the past and now we are here again back with the cub in the darkest of nights, all alone. The dream of the raging waters disturbed him and he wondered, hoping against hope. He turned over onto his side and tried to sleep, but couldn't.

Sleepless, he heard the sounds of the night: the hooting owl, the crickets, the winds in trees, and a coyote yipping far off in the distance. This was his home, and yet it was a prison without bars.

Suddenly, he heard a snap, crackle, and a thud. There were footsteps of something large not far off. Fear gripped the cub's heart, and he stood up in the starry night with moonlight shining down. He looked.

Something large was coming his way.

"Who is there?" The cub shouted, "Stay away or I will hurt you!" But in his heart, he thought, "I am small. Maybe I can scare him off."

A large form rose and bellowed a huge "ROAR!" and it hugged the cub, gripping him and wrapping its arms around him. It was an eternal embrace that didn't want to let go.

The cub cried out, and soon a wrestling match began. The cub wrestled this beast, which was easily four times his size. With move after move, the slips of the arms and the legs, it was a great match.

Every time the cub thought he had him and would win, the beast again would slip out. This went on all night long. The fire inside of the cub grew hotter and hotter. Great strength rose within him. And while he wrestled, a thought came to his mind, "Is what I wrestle my enemy or my friend? Surely he would have destroyed me by now."

And every time in this great wrestling match, the cub tried to see the beast's face. And yet he couldn't, for the darkness covered him. Just as soon as he thought he would see the face in the moonlight — that too would slip away.

Soon, before the dawn, the beast realized that "Fire Bear" would not give up. For the fire within him rose, and the anger remained.

The beast stopped moving and held the cub on his back with all limbs pinned down. He had him at last.

The beast asked, "What do you want from me?"

The young cub held his breath. Fear and courage fought in his heart as he thought of what to say.

"I want my freedom from this prison." And he still could not see the beast's face.

The beast answered, "And freedom you shall have. Where do you want to go? What will you do with this freedom?"

The cub answered, "I want to go home and get fish for my family. We are all hungry."

The beast held him down and was quiet for a moment. What was he thinking?

But the cub said with a firm voice, "And do not let me go unless you bless me."

The beast asked, "Who are you? How can I bless you unless I know your name?"

The cub replied, "I am... I am the Fire Bear who drew fish from the waters. I am here to feed the world!"

The beast replied, "Then your name must be: Andrew.... Why? For you drew and drew and drew and drew many fish from the waters. You shall prosper and be enlightened in the Spirit of the forest. For a time you had no fish. But soon you shall draw fish from the waters and give strength to your friends."

The beast released the cub and danced, bounced, and even leaped into the air. He sang over the Fire Bear Andrew and spun around singing, "And he drew and drew and drew and drew great fish and gave strength to his friends!"

The beast danced and leaped and then faded away into the darkness. "And he drew, and drew and drew great fish and gave strength to his friends." Soon the singing faded away and the sounds of the night returned.

But the song remained in the mighty Fire Bear's heart, "And he drew and he drew...... and he gave strength to his friends."

Now, something changed on the inside of the mighty Fire Bear's heart. Yes, the fire remained, but the anger was gone. Something special just happened as he wrestled the beast. But the singing and the dancing overwhelmed him. Just who was that beast, anyway?

And then the dawn came.

The Fire Bear leaped and came out of the forest. Off in the

distance was the badger, the weasel, and the raccoon. They moved along the forest floor laughing and were being just plain silly. They still laughed, remembering about the cub. "What do you think? Will we ever see him again? It's been days, months, could it even be a year?" They mocked and laughed about the cub who could not catch his fish.

But the badger, the weasel, and the raccoon smelled something. And it smelled delicious. Off in the short distance were cookies, cake, and candy, sitting a bit high above the grass on a tree stump.

Delighted, the badger, the weasel, and the raccoon saw it, and they drooled, smacking their lips. "What is this?" they thought. "Could it be a special treat just for them?"

But the Fire Bear saw the situation from another angle. Just twenty feet away, hiding behind a tree, were two hunters dressed in orange camouflage jackets and hats. And they watched the badger, the weasel, and the raccoon stepping closer to the goodies. "Could this be a good thing?" thought the Fire Bear.

Well, the badger, the weasel, and the raccoon stood before the goodies and took a swipe at the food.

SNAP! SNAP! SNAP! A wire cage wrapped around and trapped them.

The hunters came from their hiding place. And they were laughing, "Ah HA! We've got them now!" they cried.

Fear overcame the badger, the weasel, and the raccoon. They cried out, "Help! Help!" They squirmed in their cage.

The hunters came up with their guns drawn and suddenly, ROAR!!! The Fire Bear leaped in front of the hunters to stop them from hurting the badger, the weasel, and the raccoon. Fear filled the hearts of the hunters, and one of them pulled his trigger and fired his gun.

BOOM!

In slow motion, as if time stood still, the bullet flew through the air, spinning. It struck the Fire Bear in the chest, and he fell down with a thud to the ground. And yet a great roar again came out of the Fire Bear. The fire within him shouted aloud.

And even though he fell down, the roar of the Fire Bear shook the hunters and they ran away and never came back.

The forest was quiet for a moment. The badger, the weasel, and the raccoon stared at the Fire Bear lying on the ground.

They thought, "Could this be the cub they made fun of? Now he has grown and stood taller than they. He is easily four times their height."

And they felt sad. This cub, who was now a mighty grizzly bear, saved them and he died for them. How could they repay him back? A tear fell from each of their eyes. Their price would be too high. It would be impossible for them to repay.

But a rustle in the grass came. The feet of the Fire Bear moved and stirred. Life seemed to come back to him. The Fire Bear sat up!

He looked around and saw the badger, the weasel and the raccoon still stuck in their cage. The weasel cried out, "How can you still be alive!?!?"

The Fire Bear grabbed his chest and pulled a bullet out of his thick hair. There was no blood. There was no true death. There was no harm! Why? For when the Fire Bear grew up, he grew a thicker skin, and now not even a bullet could pierce his heart.

Great joy filled the hearts of the three friends. And the Fire Bear released them from their cage. They leaped, they shouted, and they cheered as the three friends thanked the mighty Fire

Bear. They couldn't stop telling him how great he was.

That afternoon, the Fire Bear stood at the bank of the river with his friends. He dipped his paws into the waters and drew and drew and drew great fish and gave them to his friends.

And just when they thought they had eaten too much and still had more fish to eat, someone new came down the river's bank. It was the cub's — excuse me (that's not correct) — the mighty Fire Bear's mother bear and father bear. They finally returned to each other and created a new home. The mother bear and the father bear loved the mighty Fire Bear. They rejoiced that they had found each other once again.

Inceptio

THE NEW KID

Odne day at school, in the afternoon, the New Kid showed up for class. She was late. Her backpack had a broken zipper, and she didn't have her books or notepads altogether. She was — let's be honest — she was a mess.

Her hair was unkempt and her face showed that she was not happy to be there. Once again, she was the New Kid. This was another turn at another school, and she wondered again if she would have a friend — any friend at that.

Well, the rest of the class was a riot, loud and ornery that the poor, poor teacher didn't know what to do. She yelled out, "Please sit down! Please get your pencils and books together! Please! Please! Please!"

But the children would play and throw papers and create havoc by doing many unruly things. The teacher wanted to quit that day.

Now, would any of you have behaved that way? Have you ever acted that way in class? I don't know, but listen, for there is a deeper story to tell here.

The New Kid walked in and she took her seat as the teacher sighed and just told her to find an empty desk.

The New Kid sat down and she pulled out an apple, for she didn't have breakfast that day. She took a nibble and felt bad because people noticed her eating. So, she put it away so that no one would take it from her.

But sitting beside her was Maddie. Maddie had her brand-new notebook and fashionable pencils. Her lunch was sitting in her bag, and it was full of goodies.

Maddie loved school and enjoyed the many moments on the playground with her friends. Every day, pretty much, was a good day. But today was more special than all the others before. But it wouldn't happen at school, at least — not yet.

The day went on, the teachers taught, the boys fought, and the classes ended. Everyone was tired and wanted to go home.

Maddie saw the New Kid walking away from the school building and down the sidewalk. There was no bus for her. There was no car to pick her up. She had to walk home from school.

Maddie stood in front of the school and looked up into the sky. The sun was shining and birds flew. Clouds dotted the sky.

Maddie said a little prayer. "Papa, can you please help the New Kid? I wish there was something we could do."

Maddie stepped forward and everything stopped in a rush! The birds held in midair. The flag on the flagpole held frozen in the wind. The children were all still, and the world had stopped for Maddie.

But the New Kid was gone, for she had just turned the corner of the street.

But Maddie could somehow move her feet. Her hair was still flowing, and she saw that everyone had stopped in time but her.

Bright light and swirls of wind came around her and lifted her up into the air. Maddie didn't know what was going on. As she flew up into the air and spun around, she looked down and saw that her body was still standing, frozen on the ground below her.

Something alarmed Maddie. Was she dead? What was happening? What was the Spirit doing in this moment?

The bright swirls of light took her higher and higher as she flew over the neighborhood and over the buildings below. She even flew past a tall office building with shiny windows. As she flew by, she saw, reflected in the windows, the slight glow of swirls. But she wasn't there, she was invisible. Maddie was caught up in the realm of the Spirit.

In a flash, Maddie stood in front of a large, run-down house. The sun stood still, frozen in the sky, and all things were still. But, in another flash, everything went backward. Zip! Flash! Whoosh!

The sun flew backward in the sky. The clouds flew backward, and the sun reversed and went down below into the horizon, and it became night. The moon zipped back in the wrong direction in the sky as the stars spun around. And again and again, the whole time rotated backward at least seven times. Light and darkness spun around.

And Maddie still stood in front of the house. And the spinning stopped. It was morning.

A large station wagon pulled up to the house full of furniture, boxes, and clothes. The Dad hopped out and yelled at the three children. One of them was the New Kid.

All three children worked hard and unloaded boxes after boxes from the car and brought them to the house while the Dad stood there and smoked a cigarette. While his children worked, only the furniture remained. They could not lift it. The Dad threw his cigarette to the ground and smashed the butt. With a huff of anger, he picked up the furniture and carried it into the house.

Maddie was invisible. No one could see her. But she saw everything. In this moment, she could see what life the New Kid lived.

Maddie cried, "She has it so hard. I wish I could help her."

And the entire world spun again. While it was spinning and the day and the night started forward again, we came to about five days later and the swirls of light and wind picked up Maddie high into the air.

She flew all over the neighborhood and came to the Grocery Store in the daytime.

Maddie saw the New Kid pushing a cart full of some groceries while the Dad complained to a driver who pushed a cart into his beat-up station wagon.

The three kids picked up the groceries and put them into the car. The New Kid picked up an apple, and she took a bite. The Dad saw this and yelled, "Wait for dinner!" He slammed the car doors shut, and they drove off in a rush.

Maddie could hear the girl's stomach growling. She thought, "I must cook her dinner!"

And again the world spun and light and darkness, day and night, the whole sky shifted and changed. The glowing swirls of light picked up Maddie again. She flew higher and higher, and up and down and around.

The day was spinning and slowed down just as Maddie floated down in front of a beautiful store.

It was a wonderful business full of many items, candy, school supplies, sodas, medicine, magazines, and newspapers. It was quite convenient.

And with a thud and a jingle, Maddie found in her pocket coins and some cash. It was $15 dollars! There were quarters, several dollar bills, and a $10 dollar bill. She was rich! — rich for a little girl!

And then a sweet smell came from inside the store. It was the wonderful aroma of popcorn and caramel candy. Someone was making dessert at the food bar.

Maddie went inside. She saw all the items. It was a gold mine of opportunity. She walked up and down the aisles, seeing all sorts of things she could buy. Maddie couldn't decide. The many choices overwhelmed her.

Down the aisle, she saw a mother and her son who was of kindergarten age. The boy grabbed a bright candy bar and tried to open it. But his mother stopped him and had him put it back on the shelf. "Here," she said, "Drink your apple juice. I'll cook you dinner when we get home."

Maddie thought about this. She had $15 and she could do whatever she wished, whatever she wanted. Why? But didn't it appear in her pocket? That's quite a trick, isn't it? A huge fortune that came her way. Wouldn't it be good to use it? But How?

Maddie went back down the aisles and found a bunch of notebooks and pencils. She picked out the pretty ones, three in fact, and a box of the best pencils. She grabbed a pencil sharpener and a box of crayons.

Down another aisle, she found a comb and some hairspray, the good, but cheap kind. She also found a small pocket mirror that was the same color as the comb. It was a perfect match.

She calculated the total cost of her items and found that she had still $3 leftover.

Maddie looked up and saw at the food counter a sign that said, "Ham and cheese sandwich with chips and drink, $4.50."

Maddie frowned. Somehow, she didn't have enough. What could she do?

The person at the counter was busy. There was a line for the people who wanted his popcorn and caramel candy, and boy, did it smell good!

Maddie felt something rise inside of her. She stepped up to the front of the line and spoke to the Counterman.

"Excuse me, sir, I have $3. Is there any sandwich you could give me for that amount? I need to eat my lunch."

The Counterman didn't see her; he was too busy bagging popcorn. And someone in line yelled, "Hey! That girl cut the line — she's not supposed to be there."

This got the Counterman's attention, "Hey little girl, go back to the end of the line."

"But, sir," said Maddie, "Can you get me a sandwich? I only have $3 dollars."

The people in the crowd got angry and their faces were showing it. They grumbled and ground their teeth. Maddie wasn't sure what to do, but she determined to make a deal.

The Counterman answered, "Listen, little girl. Can't you see I am busy? Why don't you come back another time, eh? I got a lot of work to do."

Maddie stood her ground. "I know I cut in line, but this is important. The food isn't for me."

Well, the elderly couple that stood behind her spoke up, "Hey Counterman, give her whatever she wants. She's a good little girl."

The crowd built in pressure and the Counterman gave in. "All right! All right! Here, take a sandwich, chips, and why don't you have some of this caramel candy. I got enough anyway. Now get out of here, kid. You're bothering me."

Maddie slapped the $3 onto the counter and took the food. She paid for the rest of the items and shot out of the store into the parking lot.

And as she was running, she flew up in the air with her stuff. It was one more day before her release to be in the Spirit. The sunset, and the moon flew across the sky. The stars spun and soon the sun rose in a beautiful light.

Maddie flew and saw her Mom's car driving down the street below. It was her Mom's morning drive to take her to school.

Maddie flew down and landed right back into her body in the car while her Mom talked on the cell phone.

She's back. Everything seemed normal. It felt like any other day. But this time she knew what would happen before she experienced it. She knew when the light would turn green. She knew when the car across the street would almost hit the dump truck. It was all predictable.

But she saw something she didn't noticed before. It was the New Kid walking down the street. And they were at least four miles from school.

Maddie cried out, "Stop the car, Mom! Stop the car!" "Honey, I am on the phone and we'll be late. What's wrong?" "Mom! Mom! Quick, pull off over there."

Mom was a little upset, but she did what Maddie asked, "Do you need to throw up?"

Mom pulled the car over to the sidewalk just as the New Kid walked by. Maddie called out, "Hey you!"

The New Kid stopped and was uncomfortable. "What? What do

you want?"

Maddie smiled. "You're going to the school down the road, right? I think I know you. You're the New Kid, right? Want a ride?"

Mom objected, but Maddie said, "It's ok, Mom, I know all about her."

The New Kid stepped up and looked at Maddie, who just smiled. "Sure. Thanks."

The New Kid stepped inside, sat down, and buckled up. Maddie smiled. "I know it's a long way to school. It would take you hours to get there!"

The New Kid laughed, embarrassed, "My Dad had to go to work on the other side of town."

Maddie looked down at her backpack. Inside were still all the other items she bought at the store.

Maddie asked the New Kid, "Hey! I have these things to share, you might need them." She opened her backpack and showed the New Kid.

"Oh No! I couldn't! You can't give that. I don't deserve it."

Maddie answered, "Listen, you have no idea how I got these for you."

"But how did you know?"

Maddie smiled, "I guess time will tell." Maddie paused and pulled out an apple from the backpack.

"Why don't we have some breakfast? Because you are the apple of my eye."

The New Kid took a big bite of the apple and juice ran down her face as Maddie laughed, full of joy.

Soon Maddie and the New Kid arrived at school. The kids were still rowdy. The teachers were still overwhelmed. Everything seemed crazy, but Maddie made a new friend and everyone welcomed the New Kid into the school.

Inceptio

FOUR YOUNG BOYS

F our young boys, wild and rascals they were, always vented about their chores and duties at home. Oh, how Daniel, Matthew, Evan, and Jonathan wished to escape and go to the Land of the Dragons. Fighting and swishing their swords. Together they played — hoping that someday a Mighty Knight may come their way.

One afternoon, the four young boys shut themselves up in the house during a terrible rainstorm. No one else was home; they could not find Mom and Dad anywhere. The girls? NAH — they don't like girls. But, thunder and lightning crashed! Blinded by the light and deafened by the sound, the four of them shuddered and ran into the closet in the kitchen, shivering in fear.

The rain poured outside and one of them looked out the window and saw a large shadow cross before the screen.

"Ah!" they gasped under their breath, trying to keep silent.

"What was it?"

"I don't know."

"Please call Mom and Dad," the other whimpered.

They stepped out into the kitchen. Creak, creak, creak went

the floor. Snap! Bang! Crash! Above the kitchen sink, the window broke as a tree branch pierced through the windowpane.

The boys screamed, and the shadow once again blew by the door. Whoosh! They shivered in fear and saw that the rain was coming through the window and pouring onto the counter. The boys groaned because they knew that their parents would think they were roughhousing and broke the window themselves.

"What do we do?" they asked. "Mom and Dad will ground us for sure!"

Evan stood up, for there was fire in his bones. "We didn't do it! WE know that. We must fight whatever is causing this great wind and rain."

Jonathan agreed. "Yeah, let's brave the elements."

So, together, the four boys stood up, grabbed their coats, and went out onto the porch.

The wind howled, and the rain blew and poured. They couldn't see well and wondered if they would ever come back alive. Would their parents believe the story they would tell when they return? Would anyone believe the journey they would go on?

They will believe, but they did not understand what they would see or who they would meet. That's why they call it "adventure."

They stood outside, away from the house, in the pouring rain. Lightning flashed and thunder crashed! BOOM!

And, standing before them by the big tree with their treehouse, was the Great Knight!

He stood tall with great purple feathers in his helmet and a strong sword that was four and a half feet long. Rock and slate plated his armor. Iron and steel made up his bones, and he was stronger than an ox. Diamonds and rubies adorned his breastplate, and fire came out of his shield.

This was the Mighty Knight that Jonathan dreamed of. The flaming light coming out of his helmet was this knight's face. He was terrible and mighty, but he knew there was no darkness in him.

The boys stood still, frozen in fear. The Knight stepped forward and kneeled before the four boys.

"I have come to serve you with great purpose," he said. "I am here to give you four gifts that each of you must receive and use — if you want to live."

Jonathan shivered. "What could it be?" he thought. "What does this mighty being want to give?" He thought, "I would serve him, not him, me!"

The Knight stood up and came to Jonathan and pulled from behind his shield: A pair of eyeglasses.

"These are for you to see with, dear Jonathan. See with these and you will know what to do and where to go and 'The Plan' will be before you before the day begins. These eyeglasses will help you see into the future and they will show you the enemy's schemes and strategies. Use them, and you will see how to fight. Remember that these nasty devils fear you and you can stop them and thwart them with these."

Jonathan grabbed them and looked. They didn't seem that special, they looked ordinary, but he put them on. A light shown in his imagination! Bright things swirled in his mind. He could see far beyond the mountains. He saw the dragons spewing their breath and causing all the rain and the wind. He knew that if he could find them, he could stop the nasty precipitation.

The Knight stood before Evan. From behind his breastplate, he pulled out a hot coal of fire like you would see in a campground fire pit. The coal burned hot and bright; Evan didn't know what to do.

His eyes glowed as the Knight passed it in front of him.

The Knight said to him, "Inside of you is great fire, fire that burns with great passion. The Great King is proud of you and your passion to believe in battle. Take this hot coal, and it will satisfy you. And it will bring about the energy you need to fight and stand in the battle. Wherever you go and whatever you do, know: you can do it. This hot coal is your potential. This fire burns forever, but don't quench it, for there is more to see inside of you. Take this hot coal and swallow it and it will be as honey and sweetness in your mouth. And as you eat it, it will become the vision within you."

Evan didn't know what to think. "How could he eat this? It's hot!" But he heard the knight's words and knew them to be true. If he ate this hot coal, it would produce in him passion for his fellow warriors so he may never lose heart in battle and even sacrifice for them.

Evan mustered up every bit of strength he had and took the coal. With his eyes closed, he put it in his mouth and swallowed. Soon it was tasty and delightful. "How wonderful!" he thought. "Sweet!! MMMMM."

Then the Knight came to Daniel. From underneath his helmet's visor came great light! Blinding light shone out and Daniel covered his eyes. Out of the helmet, the knight produced a diamond, a beautiful rock. He handed it to Daniel.

"My warrior, you are a gem, a precious stone. And I have given you a key to my Kingdom."

Then the knight took the stone and put it into the handle of the beautiful key.

"What the Mighty King will show you will unlock all the treasures in the people's hearts. This key will help you reveal the treasures within them. While Jonathan can see the battle plans, you can see the treasures in the hearts of all the people you meet. Use it well and be careful how you speak, but notice I have given you great wealth in this and you will find the treasure in all things."

The Knight handed the key to Daniel and placed it in his hand. As soon as Daniel touched the key, he saw in his three friends, gold and silver inside their hearts. And this would become an even greater measure of treasure. He saw inside of them the stories they would tell and the places they would go. He saw their future battles and saw that though they were great in battle and faced many challenges, he would love them through any difficulty, through thick and thin. And then he saw these three young men speak back to him and thank him for all the love and encouragement he gave over the years.

The Great and Mighty Knight came to Matthew. From underneath the sole of his foot, he produced a napkin. But it wasn't dirty! It was clean and beautiful, a pure white.

"Don't think this treasure means nothing to you or anybody else because it seems so simple and comes from a humble place. But this treasure can bring great healing to you and your heart, and those around you who are hurting. Place this napkin on your face when you lie down and rest. Breathe into it and my healing power will come and bring life where they need it."

The Knight took the napkin and placed it on his helmet's face and blew into it. It popped up and flew into the air. Matthew jumped and snatched the napkin as it floated down.

As soon as Matthew held it, he felt its soft fabric and healing power. His hand felt cool and hot at the same time. Inside this cloth was the healing power he needed. Why? Because the afternoon rain showers gave him a nasty cold and a running nose. He felt better, and his eyesight was much clearer. He could breathe again and soon he saw that if he used this napkin, he could make anyone well. In fact, he felt so confident, and he knew he could also heal their hearts.

The thunder rumbled, and the clouds grew darker and thicker. The rain poured again, and the wind blew. The Knight stood up and grew tall, taller than before. He rose high into the air. Maybe fourteen or fifteen feet or more!

The four boys shook and stepped back in fear. "What was going on?" Crash! Lightning struck and the treehouse before them shone with great light.

The Great Knight stood before the boys and declared, "Listen! Listen to your heart! There is now a voice and treasure coming unto you, and you shall see it, you shall hear it, and you shall know it. It is a voice that will help you, guide you, and tell you, 'I love you.' And this voice, when you hear it, will let you know what to do when you need help and will speak to you about these gifts I have given you."

"The Voice says to you and those who will listen, 'Come and expect me to speak to you. Come and let me show you the way. I will reveal my treasure in my heart and give you my Kingdom.'"

The wind blew hard as these four young boys stood strong with the Great Knight. Light and power swirled around them, and the Great Knight disappeared. Crash! And a clap of thunder echoed through the neighborhood.

The rain stopped, and the wind blew no more. All around them were wet leaves, the sidewalk, and the grass.

They all looked at each other. Could what they've just seen have been real? Would anyone believe them?

"The adventure is just beginning," said Evan to Jonathan. They knew it had happened, and they kept it to themselves. It was their secret to share.

They all ran back to the porch and through the door into the kitchen, full of great excitement. Daniel looked and saw the window. "Hey! It's not broken," he said. Somehow they would not be in trouble after all!

Matthew reminded them. "But remember, we gotta listen. Soon he'll speak to us again. I can't wait to find out!"

"Yeah!" they all cried with excitement. "Come on!"

The boys ran into the living room and played on their Playstation. Soon, they will go on another adventure. As they played their games, they dreamed about what the Great Knight said to them. "What does it look like? Where will they go? How will they do it? What will this voice say?"

Jonathan smiled, thinking, "I don't know, but I can't wait to fight those dragons."

Inceptio

OCEAN'S VISION

"What lies have been told as this story unfolds? But welcome me, and you shall find your heart."

Today was a great day; unlike any other. Today was the dawning of a new sunrise; fresh air sparkled in the sunlight, and he breathed it in. The great father was calling his son, and he stepped forward into the deep waters. For it was the great ocean before him, deep and wide, far and high. He knew that if he dove in, it would overtake him, but he questioned the path; the waves kept crashing and smashing against the seashore.

Over and over the waves crashed, but farther out, into the deep, he knew there was a greater story. You see, it was storytelling that beats within his heart. He knew there was a great story written on the scroll of his heart that called to him.

He was from the mountains, high in the Cascades. He loved the waterfalls, the brooks, and the mountain valleys. This was his home, and his heart was there for a time, but soon the ocean called him.

In his sleep, in the thoughtless nights, a single word kept coming to his mind. It tried to penetrate his heart, but he would not allow it. The word was pain. He saw things with his eyes that caused grief and anger, but there were some things too hard, too painful, and too grievous that he shut out and would not let in. And it was this word that haunted him night after night.

He got up in the middle of the night to look up at the moon. It shone brightly on the quiet darkness of the city. He felt lonely and thought about all the men who went to the moon. He thought it was a great adventure and a great feat, but how lonely it must be on the moon.

"Would all of this adventure, would all of this energy be worth it?" he thought. "But can I find a home? Would there be a place that would welcome me and I could call my own?"

Night after night, the cycle of the moon passed the dark skies. And again the word of pain echoed in his mind. Things he tried to shut out kept knocking and no one would know because no one would hear. "Can someone just listen!? Can someone just hear me?" he asked.

The vision of the ocean beckoned him again. He got up early and went to the shores. Off in the distance was a ship, great and glorious, full of wind in its sails. He thought how beautiful the sunrise on such a ship must be.

"What would it be like to be out there?" He kept asking because the life he sees there is grand. It is without the pain that knocks at his heart.

"Over there," he thought, "they would welcome me, and I would find a home." But he stared at the crashing waves. Over and over it taunted him. He left the beach and returned to his room.

Books were all over the floor. Reading and seeking, seeking and reading, "What wisdom may answer my questions?" he asked. There was another word that came to him. It was like a little bird, a little yellow bird that landed on the windowsill. It was beautiful. A song came out of its mouth and it sang, "My life shall overtake you, for I am pursuing you, and I sing over you night after night while you sleep! Sing! Sing! Sing!" the bird cried out, the promise cried out. This little bird sang its heart out and he listened.

The tune warmed his heart, and hope came to him. He opened the door to his place and strode out. People soon came to him and joined him down the street. It was a parade and it was for him!

Celebrations broke out and the people cheered, and the little bird, the little promise, swept around him and sang out, "My life shall overtake you, for I am pursuing you, and I sing over you day after day while you walk. Sing! Sing! Sing!" the little bird, the promise, cried out.

Life rose within him, and the celebrations overwhelmed him. New people came to him and spoke of the future, and of the things he had never heard of before. Life looked different, and life took him once again to the great ocean.

But this time, the people were there and drew a line in the sand. No, it wasn't a dare to cross this border, but an aisle, a red carpet, a path out to the great ocean. They stood on both sides and led the way to the waters. They cheered him on and shouted and said, "Hurrah! The ocean welcomes its son!"

He stood at the edge of the waters. The waves kept crashing over and over. The sun shone and again, the ship off in the distance sailed with wind in its sails. It rocked and then eased upon the waters. Life drew him into the water.

No longer would there be lies that deceived him. No longer would there be pain, because now he has dived into the deep.

Water rushed around him and people jumped in with him, swimming around him. He surfaced, and the waters became still. He swam out and looked around. The people just smiled and watched over him as the great ship sailed by.

A rope came down, and he climbed as the Captain pulled him up and out of the deep.

"Yes, my son. How great you are to see me face to face. Did you hear me singing?"

"But what about the moon? What about the pain that knocks at my heart? Will I find a home?"

The Captain took him to the bridge of the ship and the Captain steered.

"Let me show you your new home."

The ship sailed, and it picked up speed — incredible speed. The ship raced over the waters and flew and took to the air. The ship sailed higher and higher as the sun beat down. It was wonderful, it was glorious, and the sails strained at its great speed.

The ship flew beyond the ocean, the deep, and came back to fly high over the land and come to the mountains. Soon they reached the Cascades and the mountain home.

The ship floated down and came to a large wooden platform. A staircase stepped out and the man and his Captain walked down.

The light was glorious and golden. The grass was as green as could be. Snow-covered the mountains and rocks, gray as they were, stood strong and kept the mountains tall.

The Captain led him to a house, a wooden house with a few windows in it.

This was the house where the pain came to him. Fear and shame overtook his heart, his knees buckled, and he dropped in fear. Tears of grief came over him. His heart cried out, "I thought you brought me to my new home!"

The Captain knelt down beside him and wept too. "I knew that this hurt you. I knew that they didn't see you, understand you or know you. And they called themselves 'family'. But, I saw you and I had to take you back here, not to destroy you, but to redeem you. I am going inside. Will you join me?"

The Captain stood up and went to the door of the house and opened it. It took all the strength inside of him just to open his eyes. He opened his eyes and saw the Captain standing at the door with tears stinging his vision. And yet, with a quick decision, he stood up. With each step forward, it appeared an eternity took place, but with each step, he sped up.

Up the wooden steps, he entered the doorway to the house. Inside, the kitchen looked as normal as it ever did. The home and the hearth smelled just the same. But sitting at the table was the father he didn't fully know. No, it wasn't the Captain, but his father from his world.

"I am sorry, my son, I didn't see you in your youth. I knew that there were desires within you that I found strange. But I have come back to you and I have seen you and your future and I am glad. You have made me proud, though I didn't say it at the time. I know I hurt you and I am sorry, so very sorry. You are a great man and you have great strength."

The father stood up, took his hand and kissed it. "I honor you with everything in me. Will you find it in your heart to forgive as I now see you as you are?"

Tears, again, welled up within his eyes and a breaking happened. His heart broke and a great release came from within him. He released the ocean at last and life overtook him. He never knew this before. He never knew that healing would be so great.

The father and the home in front of him dissolved, and he stood back on the ship with the Captain, who stepped forward.

He asked, "Can that be real? Can that be true?"

The Captain turned the steering wheel. "More than you can ever know."

They sailed farther, and a quiet breeze flowed in his hair. While it was intense, the ocean was peaceful.

"Where are we going?" he asked.

The Captain stepped forward and gave him his spyglass. "Take a look. In it, you see my secrets."

He took the spyglass and looked out at the horizon. Inside the vision of the spyglass, he saw himself standing with honor and praise before his peers, holding many awards. His car was paid for. His home was paid for. His life was whole again. And standing with him were his friends who honored him with great strength and praise.

He put the spyglass down. "You can't be joking. That is too good. How can you do this for me?"

"But," the Captain said, "Are you not my child, my son? I see good things about you, great things. You are not ordinary. I wrote you on my heart and I welcome you there. All you need to do is ask of me and believe that I am good and that I can make your heart good. Nothing could be simpler."

He put the spyglass up again and looked out. He saw nations coming to him, wanting his stories. A new pen came to his hand and ink oozed out onto the scrolls as he madly wrote away. He was another writer of the stories of the nations. People continued to come to him and seek him for his love and wisdom. He put the spyglass down.

"How can this be? Why do they seek me?"

"Well," laughed the Captain, "When you see I have written your story and rewritten the past, fixing it up, you see you have my heart within you, and out of that abundance, you help others know their story. Welcome me, and you welcome the nations into my heart.

Today is a new day for you, my son. Welcome me, and I welcome you."

He thought this was too great. He thought secrets were evil and meant to stay hidden, but now, he found his heart and discovered that Captain can make it good.

He stood up at the bow and looked out as the ship sailed forward. Would he be king of the world? Not exactly as he imagined, but he is a king and a great one at that.

He turned back and cried out to the Captain. "Take me wherever you like! Steer and lead the way. Bring me to my future, I have seen myself there. Wholeness and life are where I am headed. Thank you for sending me the promise, that beautiful little bird. Sing! Sing! Sing! Life has overtaken me! It sings night after night, day after day and welcomes me home."

The great ship sailed on the ocean deep. The sun set and the moon came out. He looked up and saw he wasn't lonely anymore, and his heart was new and fresh. The air was delightful and flowed in his hair. He looked out and saw that the moon and the night were no longer his prison, but his sanctuary. For this day, he saw that his life was good at last.

Inceptio

THE WISDOM OF THE TREES

Long ago, in the forest of love and wisdom, were a series of trees in a circle that surrounded a deep well. Lovers and friends of the King would come out at night and seek the presence and fragrance of the trees as they made their wishes and dropped coins into the deep well. The stars always shined brightly at night about this forest, and during the day the sunlight was shining and pleasant. Sometimes storms would come, but only a slight, refreshing dew from heaven would glisten upon the green grass.

This forest is ancient and full of experience and wisdom. There are many trees here that have thick trunks and branches. They grew over a long period and their roots are deep. They are the ancient ones and inside this deep well are waters of life and refreshment. It is here that we meet the desires of the heart, and love pours out like a fountain.

The people would come and drop their coins, their heart's desires, and wish for the better things in life, the eternal things. And the trees would listen to their words. For though the trees always stood around and no one seemed to notice them, they heard every word, saw every teardrop and every broken heart that came their way.

The trees loved the people and wanted to impart more things to them, but the waters of the well would speak to the people instead. The trees have been around since the beginning of time and their roots serve the land, the earth, and their fruits drop during the right seasons to the people.

Few of these people ever know the trees, for they take them for granted. But when the wind blows and there is a stirring in the atmosphere, the music coming from the rustle of leaves; it causes such a wonderful commotion that the people long for more from the heavens.

It is the wisdom of the trees that carry the words from the well. They do not speak on their own accord but draw upon the deep waters from within the earth. Sometimes the well overflows and spills out upon the land and the people love it when that happens, but the trees long for more. They look at the people and hope that their fruits bring healing and life.

The wisdom of the trees is to never draw attention to themselves but to let fruit grow on their branches. Each tree is different and carries different fruits. They even have different smells and their leaves are unique. There is no tree identical to the next one.

Sometimes the people who come to visit the well in the forest sit under a tree and enjoy its shade and shadow. They even can fall asleep and rest in the quiet. It is here in these dreams, in the shadow of the trees, they speak. The trees enjoy this time for here, they can whisper their wisdom and love to the people.

One morning at dawn, the people came and dropped their coins in the well. And the trees listened. But this was a new day, and the well's water overflowed upon the land. It was a huge flood and a wonderful party for the people. They splashed around and found such great fun. Life was looking a little better for the land, and the trees were in their fruit-bearing season. Here, the people soaked in the waters of the well and rested under the trees. They dreamed and dreamed and dreamed some more.

The wisdom of the trees came to them and they heard the heart of the well coming from the roots of the trees. The trees were excited and shouted in their dreams that freedom was coming to the land. No longer would the earth shake so that their houses fell to the ground. No, the trees of the forest would bring great stability. Now, watch and listen, and find yourself at the well in this forest. Find yourself at rest and drink from the well. Drop your coins down, make a wish and see and hear your dreams come true as you listen to the wisdom of the trees.

Inceptio

THE STOREHOUSE OF SECRETS

T he rain was pouring heavily on the English countryside. It was chill and miserable as Sally wandered in her mind as the chauffeur drove her down the road. The water dripped and smeared as the windshield wipers tried to clear away the precipitation.

Sally didn't want to go on this trip. The endless road bored her. The destination was a distant relative's house she had not heard of.

In the beginning, when the car picked her up from school, the chauffeur and car alarmed her because they were elegant. She didn't know this distant relative was wealthy and that he always welcomed her to come and visit.

But the drive was long, and the atmosphere was dreary. The novelty of the prosperity wore off as she sat for hours in the car. The chauffeur never said a word, and she wondered why he was always so quiet. He seemed nice enough, but not accessible in the heart. He was just doing his job.

After what seemed like days on the road, the car pulled up to a large manor on the rolling hills. It was old and made of stone and wood. It had three levels to it, and the doors were hand-carved.

As they opened the entrance and stepped inside, Sally found the smell to be musty. The chauffeur brought Sally her luggage and left it in the foyer as she looked around. Before her was a huge wooden staircase, and in opposite directions, the halls spread out. Some dim light from outside poured in. Sally stepped forward and cried out, "Hello?" and her voice echoed down the halls.

Sally turned around and saw that the chauffeur had already closed the front door. She heard the engine of the car rev up, and she ran to the window and saw that the car was pulling away.

"Hey! Where are you going? There is no one here!"

With no host to welcome her, this disappointed Sally. Even the man who didn't talk to her seemed to abandon her in this great hall of some distant relative. Frustrated, she turned around and examined the foyer.

The halls to the left and right had multiple doors, and there were windows on each end. The foyer was elaborate, and many paintings hung on the walls. They displayed many marvelous men, women, and children on them. The designs seemed to celebrate the families and the colors and smiling expressions on their faces seemed to contrast with the atmosphere.

As she stepped around, Sally noticed on the handrail of the staircase that there was a note.

"Dear Sally, how I have longed to see you here. I know we've been apart for a long time, but I have brought you here so that you may discover wonderful things. I will appear soon, but for now, I have left you milk and biscuits in the kitchen down the hall to the right. See you in a little bit."

But there was no signature. Sally thought this was strange. Who exactly brought her here? What was going on? But how could she turn down milk and biscuits? And her stomach growled and agreed with her.

Sally raced down the hallway to the right and found the kitchen. Inside were many pots and pans that hung from the ceiling, and there were at least three stoves in the wall. There were many tables and sinks and on one table there were milk and biscuits.

Oh, Sally smiled and ate. The milk was in a small pitcher and cold as if it were just from the refrigerator. The biscuits on the plate were also warm and delicious, with chocolate chips that melted in her mouth as if they were just from the oven.

Sally's curiosity grew. There was something special and pleasant about this place. She thought there was more to this manor than the natural and awful atmosphere that existed outside.

There was one more biscuit left on the plate, and Sally picked it up to eat. And yet she noticed that there was a golden envelope under it.

"Wow!" thought Sally. "What is this?"

Sally opened the gold envelope, and inside was a key with a tag on it. The tag said "Level 3". And the handle of the key was in the shape of a lion's head and the hole in the key was the mouth of the lion, as if it was roaring.

"Hold on!" she thought. "This is interesting. What a marvelous key. Level 3? What is that all about? Hmm."

Sally pondered this new discovery. It was as if someone kept leading her along, and her curiosity increased. The appearance of these clues got her imagination going. Now that the milk and biscuits filled her up, she had more energy to empower her on her way, and what else could she do but explore the manor and find out what door this key goes to?

She left the kitchen, entered the hallway and looked at all the doors. Each door was marvelous because they had different engraved panels on them. On this floor, all the panels had images of things common on the earth. Trees, People, Mountains, Rivers, Oceans, Fields of Grain, Schools, Barns, etc.

She continued down the hallway and then found herself in the foyer again. The other wings on the opposite side had more doors. Sally looked at the key again and its tag, "Level 3".

Sally realized what a simple clue it was. "Of course! I must go upstairs to the third floor."

Sally hurried her little feet and started up the staircase as it wound around up higher to the second level.

As she made her way to the landing on the second level, Sally noticed this floor was dark and dim and that there were multiple candles that lit the two wings. The mood here was difficult and uneasy. It seemed as if there were ghosts or dark things that lurked around here. The mystery of the unknown seemed to pull her away from the staircase, and her curiosity answered.

Sally, against her best judgment, looked around the hallway of this second floor. The candlelight was dim, but there was enough light to see the engravings on the doors. This time the pictures differed from the first floor. Here were images of dragons, wild beasts, sea monsters, and countless insects. There were also other images of great warriors with swords and marvelous men in battle array. Lightning bolts and thunderhead clouds filled the images above them. There were battles and skirmishes going on at all times.

At the end of the hallway was another door. On the door, the wooden engravings had gold paint on them that was peeling away as if it were old and ancient. Sally picked off the gold paint and saw it wasn't real gold at all, but the image on the door had gotten her attention.

The image showed a throne of stone and a dark cloud with bolts of lightning that shot out around it. Beneath the throne were swirls of clouds and serpents. At the top of the throne, there were words she couldn't discern their translation. But the backdrop of the image around the throne showed countless grapes and cups of wine. Sally looked closer and saw that there were many faces with mouths open. They seemed to drink from the cups of wine.

Sally wondered about this mystical and magical image. It was fantastic, and it was dark. Sally then thought, "What is behind this door?"

Sally looked down at the handle to the door and saw it was broken and cracked open a little. Red light seemed to pour out from behind the gap.

Sally then took her hand and gripped the handle. Fear rose in her throat and her heart beat more and more. The door handle clicked and clicked as she turned.

The key in the golden envelope dropped from her pocket and landed between her feet. She stopped, closed the door, and picked up the key. Just as she did, a huge roar of a lion resounded down the hallway! ROAR!

Sally gasped in fear and stood straight up. Something inside her knew this wasn't the right door. In a rush, Sally left the Door of Temptation and made her way back to the staircase. It was time to reach the third level.

Up the stairs, she ran, and she wound her way to the third-floor landing. What was surprising was that the landing didn't open to the wings from the left and right. Instead, the landing was a small room with only one door facing the opposite wall. The lighting was golden, and there was a marvelous chandelier hanging above. Gorgeous patterns of leaves that flowed vertically in lines covered the walls. It was like the interior of a ritzy hotel.

Sally stepped up to the door. The paneling of the door was smooth and simple with a dark brown wood, and it was so shiny that you could almost see Sally's reflection in it. It was like looking through a glass darkly.

The doorknob, however, was pure gold and was in the shape of a lion's head. Sally's eyes opened wide, and she pulled out the key with the handle of the lion's mouth.

As she inserted the key, a great peace came over her, and she felt like she was about to float off the floor. It was such an overwhelming sense of joy and freedom, something she hadn't ever felt before, and her fingers tingled as the key flowed forward into the lock.

With a quick twist and a turn, the door handle unlocked and swung open with the greatest of ease.

A bright light shone and wrapped around Sally. A great force of love seemed to pull her into the room. It was so bright that Sally held up her hands to her eyes as she floated forward into the source.

But Sally's eyes adjusted and she could look around and see where she was. To her delight she found that there were shelves upon shelves and rows upon rows of golden boxes of different sizes, all resting in their proper places.

Sally looked up to the ceiling and noticed that the light that shone in the place didn't come from a lamp or candles, but in fact, above her, it was a skylight, and instead of the dreary, rainy atmosphere, it was the glory of the golden sun that filled the room.

Sally stepped forward and walked around and saw that some of the golden boxes were open, with their lids hanging beside the attached case. On the front of each opened case were plaques with dates and a name written in golden handwriting.

For many of the open treasure chests, she recognized things that were familiar. For example, she saw a plaque that said, "Printing press: Johannes Gutenberg — 1436" Another said "The Wizard of Oz: Lyman Frank Baum — 1900" And another said "Theory of Relativity, Albert Einstein — 1907."

Sally smiled and realized that these were, in fact, old treasure chests that contained the marvelous revelations of great things from the past. Sally was excited, and she ran up and down the rows of shelves and saw countless old, open treasure chests.

But then she stopped and saw that there were many more up ahead that had locks that closed them shut. Could it be that there were more treasures yet to behold? Could it be that she was privy to the secrets of the universe?

Even though she was excited, she stepped forward and looked at the plaques of unopened treasures. Here she saw some of them say, "Theory of Everything," "Intergalactic Space Engine," "Reanimation of Dead Tissue," "Frictionless Bearings," "Parallel Universe Detectors," "Screenplay for the Next Generation," and on she read.

These were unclaimed treasures. These were things of powerful value and eternal influence. Sally's head was about to explode as she saw the incredible genius they contained. But what would allow her to open these boxes? What could she do to unlock the secrets of the universe? There were no names on them. There were no dates. It was as if these treasures could open up at any time and anyone could receive them.

"Amazing," thought Sally.

As she pondered, Sally realized that these items, these revelations, these treasures were so delicate and powerful that not just anyone could have them. No, these could only be given to someone who was faithful, responsible, and trustworthy enough to handle them. It was that they were so valuable that the power that comes from these treasures would change the world.

But Sally pondered even more. Some treasures that were open were given to people in the past who simply experienced a revelation and went for it. Not all of them were noble people, or ones with kind hearts. Sally peered again and saw these treasures were given without partiality. The people didn't have to have it all together. They had to have been willing to take the risk and see these things come to pass.

Sally saw that some of the unopened treasures were only possible if one combined two factors together. Yes, every treasure is valuable and honorable, and yes, some in the past were corrupt people and received the revelations, but these were the last batch of treasures that remained. These were the highest and most valuable, and these could only be given to those who were faithful. Here was the price, and here was the cost to handle them.

Sally thought hard about the possibilities. The stakes are too high in these days for people to waste these treasures. Sally wondered if she could be one of them.

She turned around and saw the wealth of the heavens before her and sighed a sigh of deep contentment. Everything was at her disposal. If the distant relative that owns this manor gave her the key to Level 3, then this was not a mistake. Something about this gift of the key with the lion's mouth helped her see she must be trustworthy. Not anyone can come to the Storehouse of Secrets. But maybe she can help others come when she finds them able and ready.

Sally found a notebook and logged many of the treasures and kept great records of what remained. Some treasures' names made little sense, but she knew given time everything would become clear. Sally determined in herself that she would be faithful to these valuables. She locked the lion door behind her and pocketed the key.

Down the stairs, she skipped and steered clear of the second floor as she found her way back to the kitchen. As she stepped inside hoping for more milk and biscuits, there was a tall man with his back toward her cooking at the stove. The delicious smell filled the air, and she was hungry for something new.

Though the man didn't show his face, he spoke and asked, "Sally, are you ready for what I am cooking up next? I can promise you, it will taste just delicious."

Sally's eyes grew large again, and she sat down at the table to dine once more. Truly, this was the best surprise she had ever experienced.

Inceptio

TIME OF DESIRE

Famished for love and longing for light,
The Woman, the creator stood strong,
as she pursued her delight.

In her hands were the scissors that carved the cloth
that kings and queens would wear,
As they walked down the aisles,
and the beauties would just stare.

People from all over the world would seek her sight,
For her designs were designs of delight.

But now, let us go back to the beginning of this desire,
When life was hot and her heart was on fire.

Inside her burned the sights and the sounds,
Of people in clothes dancing, twirling around and around.

Inside her heart was the design of delight,
And people all over the world would seek her out,
For she knew what colors, clothes, and styles were life and bright.

In the beginning, there were steps of risk, trials, and tribulations,
But favor bounded over all.

She walked down the street and entered her court.
Many saw the things she saw, and she blurted out her exhort.

Inside her eyes was a vision of the future,
and people knew that there were treasures within.
But came the question:
when would she release them and let her story begin?

People come and people go
But along the lines, she saw the design,
And saw the fabric perfectly flow.

Color, lines, styles, and delight filled her mind night after night.
For she dreamed to draw and color and cut,
But inside her was the caution that made her say "But?"

She was thoughtful and hesitant to move,
But could she live the life she dreamed of?

Inside her was the desire, yet when was the time?
When could she release and find her life to be so sublime?

What could she do and where could she go?
She wanted to release, but she was afraid to flow.

In her hands were crayons of color,

But would she fly in her heart and become like no other?
Yes, it was time, the Time of Desire.

And thoughtful people came to her and encouraged her way.
For she heard her heart and she knew what to say.

"It is time, it is time. It is time for Desire."
Now she was free and her heart was on fire.
Inside of her again she looked at the place of creativity.
She saw many things and her gift was full of productivity.

Now it was time to start a new beginning,
For the seasons have changed and now she started the winning.

Draw, draw, draw, cut fabrics of desire.
Templates, forms, sewing and then,
go to bed for the night and retire.

People will come and people will go,
But prepare yourself for you will end up with The Show.

Hide away from those who speak doubt,
Surround yourself with the people who spur you on and cheer you
and shout.

Celebration is here, now you are free;
To be everything you are to be all you can be.

Today we celebrate you and give you the freedom to live.

Believing in yourself and give yourself a break, and love to forgive.

You've been so hard on your soul and your soul cries out,
"Love me just a little and together we will enter the realms of favor and clout."

Inside of you is a great treasure, it comes from the Creator,
The Lord of Hosts who loves you with a great Measure.
You have much sight inside you, now apply your pleasure.

Come and be with the One who will inspire you for all you do.
You can do this; we believe that they will marvel your designs,
And people will want to work with you.

Fashion and favor surround you my dearest daughter.
People love you and will give you treasures that will take you farther.

Farther than you'd ever dreamt of before.
For yours is the Kingdom, more and more.

Live and love and love again.
We desperately need your heart, it is time to begin.

This is your heart song, the song of desire.
It is time, it is time. Prepare yourself and you will find your heart on fire.

We love you and honor you and keep you today.
We will surround you and pray for you and follow your way.

We love who you are and celebrate your treasure.
You have power, grace and favor, by far beyond measure.

Look out and see that your deliverance is near,
Go forward and believe there is no need for fear.

You are now released, go and be.
Do what you desire for you are now free.

Inceptio

IN THE HALL OF THE MOUNTAIN KING

Dark clouds of smoke covered the sky, and the rocks were hot like fire in the jagged mountain. The place was dark even though it was daytime. And yet the weary Warrior walked up the sharp craggy rocky trail, holding a torch in his hand as he pursued the summit. In his sheath was his sword, but he struggled to find his way through the trails on the mountain. The Warrior kept walking higher and higher up the peak, knowing that the view at the top would be spectacular.

The Warrior's journey brought him to many places and through many valleys, but there were no other mountains like this. The higher he climbed, the more difficult it was to see where he was going and how high he was. The view along the way was dangerous, with sharp rocks of beautiful, rich colors. The land had lost its once lush meadows and green forest life and now devastation ruled. Bones and dead bodies from long ago littered the trail. The skulls' eyes seemed to look out at the Warrior and taunt him. He swore he could hear their thoughts; their spirits harassing him, saying, "You shall die like the rest of us!"

But the Warrior continued his trek and tightened his belt, the truth of what held him together. Higher and higher he wound his way up the trail, back and forth, scrambling on the stage of life.

The rocks beneath his feet were loose and difficult, and he feared he would sprain his ankle. But he would not give up.

The trail seemed to stop in front of him. A tall wall of rock faced him and it was like a dead-end. The impasse seemed impossible, and that there was nothing else he could do. "Was this the end?" he thought. "What is the way through this? I cannot go forward!"

As he examined the rock wall that stretched high in the air before him, he saw runes engraved on the surface. The dark language of ancient tongues seemed to laugh at him even more. Though he could not translate it, the words seemed to haunt the mountain as if no one could live in this place and reign. It was a covenant with death.

The Warrior saw this and became furious. Howls and cries came from behind him and he turned around and looked at the source of the shrieks. Coming up behind him were the shades of the fallen that littered the trail. It was like a swirling flood of evil smoke that wound its way like a hurricane right toward him.

The Warrior stood his ground and held his torch high while he pulled out his sword. As he unsheathed his sword, electricity shot out of the torch and lit the sword with glowing blue flames. The Sword seemed to create a revelation in his eyes. He knew that as soon as he used the Sword, his torch would light his way and create a breakthrough for his situation.

The hurricane of ghosts rushed closer and their cries echoed in the mountain. The Warrior turned around and looked at the rock wall. The rocks closed him in, he thought.

But the blue flames of revelation caused a unique idea to enter his mind. With a quick move and with great strength, the Warrior took his Sword and struck the wall in front of him. The Sword pierced the stone and the ground shook.

A huge earthquake happened, and the cliffs high above loose their boulders and they fell down into the chasm of the trail. The rocks, stones, and boulders came down with such a crash they covered the ghostly horde, and peace filled the atmosphere.

The Warrior stood stunned, thinking the avalanche trapped him even more. He struck the rock, and his efforts thwarted the enemy. But would he have any hope of going anywhere else?

Yet the Warrior turned around to retrieve his Sword, and as he looked, he saw the Sword caused a crack in the wall of rock. The line of the crack ran vertically, high above into the sky, but the bottom of the crack stood before him, and there was a little hole in its end. The Warrior's eyes opened with curiosity and he inspected it. The little hole was an opening of a keyhole.

This caused the Warrior to remember the gift his Father gave him. It was a small treasure given to him long ago in his youth. The Father found the son walking along the street years ago and handed him his future, saying, "You're gonna make it, kid! You're still gonna make it!" The little treasure was a tiny key he hung on his necklace. He kept it hidden and revealed it only to a special few.

The Warrior then took it out and inserted it into the keyhole. Loud noises sang from inside the rock wall and it clunked and clanged as if there was a great unlocking.

The rock wall split into two pieces and cracked open before him. The ground shook as the path opened up and a new way to enter. The Warrior stepped forward and held his torch and sword, the sword's blue light filling the space before him.

The Warrior entered the Hall of the Mountain King.

As he went in, his eyes adjusted to the dark light. The hall was dim, but it was not impossible to see. Forms and structure became clear and he could see the rock buttresses that held the hall high. In front of him stood a large, long staircase that grew narrow as it rose. At the top was an empty throne.

Chandeliers above him glowed with candlelight and the darkness thinned. The Warrior saw the more he walked forward toward the steps of the staircase to the throne, the lighter it became.

As he walked, people appeared on the side wings of the hall. They held out hands to him, for they wanted to dance with him and spin him around, but the Warrior wouldn't because their hands were sticky. He couldn't set down his sword and torch to dance a Dance of Distraction.

The Warrior bowed before them in honor, and yet the people turned their backs from him and dishonored him since he would not dance.

Some of them spit darts of stinging poison toward him. The painful darts hurt for a moment, but he continued to walk up the staircase towards the throne. He knew that he must honor the people, for he was in the Hall of the Mountain King.

When the Warrior had made it halfway up the staircase, there appeared before him, the Wizard of the Land. The Wizard did not speak one word, but his hands came upon the Warrior's shoulders and their eyes fixed onto each other. The Wizard's eyes looked upon the Warrior with great compassion, as he could see that there was little strength left in him, but as he held him, strength filled his soul. The Warrior knew that if there was but one man who truly knew him, then there would be enough power to move on.

And so he did. He walked higher to the throne at the top of the staircase. Lighter and lighter became the hall and the rock walls and buttresses went from dark blue-gray to a lighter orange and yellow. Glory seemed to fill the place.

The Dancers of Distraction were below the Warrior, spun around as a whole as they raised their hands repeatedly, in honor of the Warrior. They saw that since his honor came their way, they did not know what to say to him. They realized that they could not control the Warrior and his hall, for they had no authority in it. They did not have the birthright, nor were they the heir. They were dancers of default, not of destiny.

And so the Warrior came to the top of the staircase and examined the throne. It was dusty and cobwebs covered it. He took his torch and burned off the dust and junk, and soon his heart purified the throne.

Sitting on the back of the throne above the head was an inscription. At first, the letters seemed too small, but as he peered, the inscriptions seemed to grow larger and bolder. It said,

"Fear of gold, fear of light, shining bright and full of delight. Let no one come to take your desire. Guard, protect, and inspire. Set them free with your spirit bright. Give them peace and stand in the fight. Now go and take your thrones. Speak the decrees and make them your own. This is your seat, this is your house. Be bold as a lion and not whimper like a mouse. Set us free with your sight. Give us your gold and shine your light."

After he read the inscription, he turned and looked down at the armrest of the throne. Sitting there was a beautiful butterfly with multiple colors on its wings. It was large, and the wings were crystal, delicate and thin. As it moved its wings, bright flashes of light pulsated out. Then a gust of wind came and blew the butterfly up as it flew high into the air and into the sunlight.

The Warrior looked out and saw the butterfly leave. It was at this moment he noticed that the throne became higher than even the halls of the mountain. He could look over to the land and out to the horizon. Darkness was fading, and the land was filled with light and the sun rose high in the sky above the throne. Blue skies and orange clouds filled the zenith, and the hall opened up more and more.

The Dancers of Distraction below then shivered in fear, for the beauty of the light caused them to remember their dishonor to the

Warrior. Though they judged him, he still sacrificed his desire to retaliate, for his calling was nobler than theirs. They then ran to his feet and kissed them and asked for his blessing. They knew they couldn't beat him, so they decided that they could join him with honor.

The Warrior sat on the Throne of the Hall of the Mountain King and ruled over the land. He did not lord over them but loved on them all. He saw he had great strength and the poisonous darts that the Dancers of Distraction shot at him became the antidotes of love. He turned them around and soon they became his vast army. Though they did not understand him or honor him, the Land promoted him, and his heart was from love and deep forgiveness. He saw that in his strength, it was greater to be compassionate than to be weak and strike down in harm.

As the Warrior who became King ruled, the land became whole. The streams were no longer bitter. The crops grew and they were very fruitful. Blindness and darkness in the land's eyes became clear, and they finally saw each other as they truly were. Treasures upon treasures appeared, and the rains returned and refreshed the fields.

And thus, the Warrior who became King kept stepping forward and didn't give up; he found his rest and peace as Love filled the land.

Inceptio

THE STORM DRAGON

O ut in the field, Bethany hopped and skipped around, looking at all the colorful ornaments of the wildflowers. She bent down, touching each one, and felt its softness. The smell was wonderful; a fragrant aroma of life filled the forest. The trees surrounding her were tall evergreens, and the mountains behind them rose high and touched the clouds.

Bethany and her family were on a trip visiting the Rocky Mountains. Bethany also had her new present, a digital camera, and took snapshot after snapshot of all the beautiful scenes. She got better and better at her photography, for she was astute at composition, lighting, and design. The ability to see in this way became a new hobby for her.

As she walked out, her parents and Jeremiah were behind her at the campground, fixing the pop tent and getting ready for dinner. Jeremiah was hurrying to get all the marshmallows, chocolate, and graham crackers for tonight's campfire. He was excited about being out in the woods. Mom and Dad wanted them to remember this trip.

Bethany continued her stroll through the field, and the clouds of a thunderstorm came overhead. The sky grew darker, and the thunderhead rose and turned a deep blue, almost purple, color.

Bethany was so far away she didn't hear her Dad calling for her to return to the campsite. The experience of the wilderness fixed her attention and focus.

But another voice spoke up. A small, delightful chirp, "Bethany! Bethany! Do you know where you are?"

She turned around and looked. She saw no one. Bethany thought it was weird to hear a voice in the forest. More curiosity came, however, as up ahead on the other side of the valley was the Lake.

Here was Eagle Lake. They called it Eagle Lake because from high in the sky it was similar in shape to a flying eagle. Many people had great stories from boating on this lake. Tourists had caught many fish in the past. Nowadays there aren't that many caught.

Bethany walked up to the sandy shore and picked up a large, palm-sized rock that was flat. Following the motion her Mom taught her, she threw the flat rock and skipped it across the water. Boop. Boop. Boop. Splash! It sunk into the waters.

As she strolled down the shoreline, the little sweet chirp came again. "Bethany! Bethany!"

Bethany stopped dead in her tracks. "Hello? What do you want?"

The small chirping voice cried out, "Bethany! Do you know where you are?"

The sound of the voice came from a large white log bleached from years of sitting in the sun. One of its old branches stuck up and sitting on it was a small robin bird. It was colorful with red on its chest and white and black wings with a reddish-orange head.

"Bethany! Do you know where you are?"

The little girl's eyes grew wide open as she walked to the bird.

"Were you talking to me, little bird? What is your name?"

The robin fluttered his wings and chirped. "I am Visionado. I am the one who sees for you. The Great King sent me to you, for you have a task at hand. Do you know where you are?"

Bethany looked concerned. Why did this bird ask if she knew where she was? "I am here at the Eagle Lake with my family camping. That's where I am."

Visionado fluttered his wings, flew down to the ground, and stood in front of her. "Yes, that is where you are in the natural world. What do you see in your heart? Why do you always go on these trips? Is it merely a vacation? What do you see?"

Now Bethany knew that Visionado asked something important. She had heard about her friends, Maddie, Katie, and Hannah, who met the Lady of the Wind. (See the story "The Three Young Girls".) That great being gave them many gifts to see. But maybe there was more.

Bethany asked, "Where do you want me to look?"

Visionado flapped his wings, took to the air, and flew above the waters of the lake. Visionado circled and brooded over the waters just like he did in the Beginning of Time. "Peer into the deep. What do you see?"

Bethany kicked off her shoes and socks and waded into the shallow waters of the Lake. Just as she stepped out, the tall dark clouds in the sky crackled with lightning and booms of thunder.

Bethany looked down into the waters. At first, she saw the mountains' reflection and the sky. As she peered more and more, though, she saw countless fish swimming around below the surface.

"I see fish inside the waters of the deep," she cried out.

Visionado flew and fluttered. "Very good! What else do you see?"

Bethany continued to look. Inside the waters, the fish that swam turned gold and shined bright like the sun. And just after that, a huge BOOM! Of thunder and lightning as the bolt struck a tree across the lake. Bethany became afraid.

"Fear not the lightning of the enemy, dear Bethany!" cautioned Visionado. "This is mere intimidation. Continue to see."

The golden fish swam around and around and soon encircled her.

"I see the fish turning to gold and they are all around me! What is going on?" asked Bethany.

"You are seeing my treasure," said the bird. "Inside the deep waters are my treasure, my desire, and my promise to the people of the World. You see my gold in the fish. At first, you saw the mountains and the storm, but as you looked deep, inside the storm you saw my treasure."

"But why do they circle and swim around me?"

Visionado landed in Bethany's hand, dancing and hopping around. "They draw near you, for you chose to walk into the deep and see for them. You have a sight and you have a voice inside of you. My voice speaks in the form of this little bird. But I want you to listen to my voice within your heart. Do you know where you are?"

Bethany held up Visionado to her eyes. "Yes. I can see now. You want me to see the fish as your treasure. And help them see too."

"Exactly," chirped the bird with cheerful delight. KABOOM! Thunder and lightning blew across the sky above them. Bethany became afraid and looked up to the sky.

Inside the dark clouds, something collected. Bethany started for the shoreline. As she ran, she looked behind her. The dark clouds spun and swirled. It wasn't a tornado, but it looked like a dark cloud in the shape of a flying dragon. This was the Storm Dragon, and it flew right after her.

Bethany let go of Visionado, who fluttered and tried to keep up. "Wait, Bethany! Wait! There is more here in the storm!"

Bethany grabbed her socks and shoes, ran back to the field of wildflowers, and tried to head back to camp. Visionado caught up and fluttered in front of her face. "Wait! Stop! Look!"

Bethany halted her run and stood her ground. She turned around, still afraid, and faced the storm. In front of her flew the dark clouds formed by the wind and the Storm Dragon snarled and moved back and forth, like a lion in a cage.

Visionado flew to Bethany's right shoulder and whispered, "This Storm Dragon will always chase you if you run, but if you stop and resist, he will retreat. Speak to the Storm Dragon."

"What do I say?" asked Bethany, with fear inside her voice.

"Speak what you saw in the deep waters. Speak the promise and identify the treasure in the Storm."

Bethany collected the images of everything she had seen. She remembered how Visionado said it was a Storm of Intimidation.

She held her hand up against the Storm Dragon. "In the Name of the Mighty King, I tell you what I saw! I saw fish in the deep, the golden treasure, and the promises of the King. I no longer saw just the mountains, I saw within the deep! Now, Storm Dragon, you must flee, for I declare this treasure to the World and you cannot chase me anymore! I stand my ground and I speak what I hear and what I see. Visionado here is my guide and I see within you, Storm Dragon, a lie. You are nothing but dust and shadows, winds of the air, and storms of the sea. You have no substance and I see within you *my opportunity* to see and to win. You cannot take this treasure. You cannot take the golden fish of the deep. They belong to the

King!"

The Storm Dragon slithered and snarled, and the clouds that made it dissolved away. The thunderheads and the dark sky returned to the sunny day, and the winds stopped. The cool air became warm and peace came to the valley of wildflowers.

Bethany's dad hopped up next to her. "Bethany! Did you hear me calling you? Where were you?"

Bethany hugged her dad and cried out, "I saw the storm and ran to you. But I could see the treasure in the Storm. Visionado helped me."

Dad took Bethany in her arms. "Visionado?" "Yes, my little bird. He spoke to me."

Bethany looked and saw the little bird fly high into the sky and into the sun. He seemed to wave back at her. But Bethany's Dad picked her up and held her in his arms. He said, "I think it's time to listen to me instead. Let Visionado help you the next time. Come on, kiddo. Jeremiah is waiting to make some S'mores."

"OK!" smiled Bethany.

And with that, father and daughter raced across the field of wildflowers to the campground and the afternoon sky became a golden red. Bethany and her family all sat in lawn chairs and watched the new fire lit in the campground. Bethany thought to herself, "What a great vacation. Do I know where I am? I am with my family. And I can see and I can hear... I do."

Inceptio

CLIFFHANGER

Frazzled, Karissa opened her eyes from an unconscious daze. The wound on her head left a large lump and she could not remember how she got to this location. Tired and worn, she stood up and looked around her.

It was dark. Her torch lay next to her and had almost lost its flame. She picked it up and looked around. Surrounding her were many columns of stone, and she saw she was inside a large catacomb of tombs. Dead, old, and dusty bodies lay in their places in carved graves in the walls.

"What in the world?" she asked. The last thing she could remember was that she was enjoying the day in Italy, in the canals of Venice, and the sun was bright and shining. She was full of pleasure because she was free from her responsibilities of school and the vacation was what she asked for.

But while she was having the most delicious coffee at the café and waiting for her blind date to arrive, the knock of calling came upon her head, and now in the darkness, she had awoken to her desire again.

She walked forward, exploring the tombs and examining the columns. Here were the dead places and the lost places. Here were the places of dreams that died. And yet, this was the place of desire, anyway. The smell was musty and stunk. Her faint torch lit the way, and she got anxious about the exit. Where is her way out?

On one column was a series of inscriptions that were in Latin. With her training and genius mind, she could translate the words, though they were difficult to make out. It was enough to say it: "Awake, O Sleeper. Your desire is the dawn."

She mumbled and muttered the words in her mouth as she tried to form the pronunciation. And as she did, the ground rumbled and shook. Something supernatural was happening. It was a small shudder in the ground, and some dust crumbled from the ceiling above her.

Out of fear that the ceiling would cave in, Karissa stopped her words and held firm onto the rock on the wall. The maze of columns left her confused still as she didn't know the way to escape. Her declaration was too difficult to utter. Even the simplest whisper of her mouth from the longings of her heart had great power. She saw she must be careful, as even the simplest voice of risk would ignite the heavens.

Off in the distance, Karissa peered and toward great darkness, there might be the exit. She thought she could see a glowing purple and blue mist of light far off in the distance. It seemed to swirl in magical color and a small orb of light. But she could not see the floor of the tomb, and the columns didn't allow her to veer to the left or to the right. She feared that the place must be unstable because of its age.

She thought to herself, "This tomb, this place, it seems too old for me to find my treasure. Has this place been all but forgotten? What and where is the way out? Is there any reward for my exploration?"

And yet Karissa saw the purple and blue mist off in the distance, still glowing. It seemed brighter.

Karissa took a deep breath and held up her torch and ran. She charged toward the glowing mist and didn't care what would happen.

Either she would find her reward and get out of the place of death and dying dreams, or she would end her journey now and know that her risk-taking was her last and final choice.

The pursuit of the mist down the columns triggered many booby traps and mechanical functions of the walls. Shrieks and screams from the left and the right cried out as the dreams and their oppressors tried to distract Karissa.

Explosions of dust and quick flames burst out. Karissa looked to her sides and saw that there were demons hiding behind the columns. They spat out of their mouths acidic poisons that almost hit her. She increased her speed and ran even harder and jumped side to side as various rock obstacles shot up from the floor of the tomb and tried to hinder her way.

The glowing purple mist came closer as she ran. It hung in the doorway and there seemed to be sunlight from high above that shone down. And there was some green moss and vines that hung on the walls. "At last!" she thought she would make a way of escape.

Just as she cleared the way, a huge rumble shook the entire tomb and a great rock wall slammed the door shut. Her torch went out. Grit and dust filled the air. Karissa choked and gagged, as she could not breathe. Even the oxygen seemed to vanish.

Next, a sound in her ears whispered. It was the voices of the demonic laughing and cackling. The words were not clear, and they seemed to mock her and delight in her darkness and despair.

Karissa looked out and reached with her arms and tried to push away the oppression, but she seemed to touch nothing.

It was the head demon of the tomb, and he spoke. "You thought you'd escape, didn't you? You thought you would be free? But no! I have you in my clutches," he laughed.

Karissa held her breath in fear. The demon moved closer to her face and gripped her throat.

She choked and struggled as her back was against the wall.

He spoke again. "You explored my territory. You saw all my secrets. You know my ways and sought to expose them, but you... have lost!"

Karissa choked even more as the demon tightened her throat. She thought this was her end. "Now... you must sleep," said the head demon.

Karissa felt drowsy, and she lost consciousness again. She nodded her head as the grip became tighter. "Yes. I must sleep. Sleep... O Sleeper. Sleep. O. O. O? Sleeper. Sleeper! Sleeper!" she cried out. Revelation hit Karissa's heart, and a light shined out of her eyes into the master of the tomb's face.

The demon screamed and loosened his grip. Karissa got a crazy and excited look on her face. She cried out in her Latin words. "Awake, O Sleeper! Awake, O Sleeper! Your desire is... Your desire is... The dawn!"

With those words, a light shone out from the cracks of the floor and burst from the seams of the rocks on the walls. The whole room glowed with an intense and increasing light from the sun.

The demons that hid in the dead bodies of dreams could not hide any longer. The light of desire exposed them. They freaked out and cried and scampered like cockroaches caught in the beams of light.

Karissa's excitement increased and her torch was full of flame.

She was back and her desire was on fire! Karissa chased the demons throughout the tomb. One by one she pierced the darkness of the demons with her torch of desire and disintegrated them into a desperate nothing.

Soon the whole room was empty of evil. The dead bodies of dreams and their bones danced and rattled. Life filled them and they glowed with the same purple and blue mist she pursued.

One by one the bodies shone out, and they came alive, and in an instant, they stood up and left their shelves in the walls.

Karissa stood strong and had a small army of dreams in front of her. Together they stood by her side by side and could do whatever she asked.

Karissa turned around and faced the huge rock wall that slammed shut and blocked her way. Her army of dreams stood beside her and waited for her next move.

She became quiet and put her ear to the rock wall and listened. Karissa closed her eyes and inhaled. Then she opened them and looked straight out and whispered. "Awake, O Sleeper! Awake!" And the huge wall shot straight up and a bright white light filled the space.

What will happen next? What is this new day for Karissa? What desire will awaken in her heart? Ahh.... my friends, these questions are why her stories will always have a 'Cliffhanger'.

Inceptio

THE KINGDOM OF TWO WELLS

O ut in the desert, on a great journey, a Man and his camel traveled upon the sands. The desert had many dunes, and the sun beat down upon the Man's hardened soul. For many miles and many days, he sought the horizon, but could never reach it. Inside, his soul was dying and was heavy with thirst.

Sometime later, the Man and his camel came alongside a large caravan of travelers. They played their musical instruments and sang aloud. He thought they were a mysterious troupe, and he wondered, "Could they be good, could they be a light? Could they bring me delight?"

He thought about their strange ways and traveled with them for a jaunt, which led to the sunset and the day's end. For now, there were fires that lit up the night sky as they camped under the moon and played their songs. The din and the dance whirled around the Man as he sat dizzily with amazement.

At camp, in the pit, the very deep pit was delicious and delectable delights of meats from wild animals from far-off lands. The band of travelers danced, sang, and tripped out around and about in the sands. They leaped in the air, for they sought the delight of the darkness and even shunned the moon and her faint light.

The Man ate and ate, and then he ate some more. And the more of the wild meats he ate, the deeper the pit in his stomach became. It was delightful for a season, but this constant barrage of sound, smell, and sight sickened his heart.

He thought he knew the voice and the language of the travelers. He thought he could teach them his native tongue, but they sought to speak to him and teach him their tongue. It was difficult for him, yet still tried to share the tongue of his former land. They couldn't hear and they shouted and laughed into the darkness, for their ears could not understand.

A gnarly traveler handed the Man a piece of meat. "Take this, my son, and I will give you your desires. Only, just... let me have some gold from your pocket and I will give you more."

The Man took the meat and paid the price with his gold and dropped it into the hands of the traveler. He leaped up into the air as he took the gold, shouted and spit on it, and then dropped it to the earth and spat on it again. He danced and danced in circles over the gold and ran away into the darkness, laughing hysterically.

And yet, the sad Man ate his rotten meat.

He fell asleep at night and awoke hours later. The fire pit had just a few coals burning, and it was dark. The moon had sunk and the sun wasn't up. It was the darkest of nights, and to his surprise, the travelers had vanished.

"Where are my friends?" he asked, and he looked around. As he got up from the desert floor, he tried to stand and saw that ropes bound his feet and both his robe and his shirt, the ones his Father gave him. Someone stripped them from his body and torn them to shreds around him.

Inside, his heart broke and cried out, for there was a deeper issue at hand. All he owned were his pants, belt, and the rope around his feet. His hands were free, but the knot on the rope was too great to untie.

How could he move? How could he walk? What could he do? His hands could work and produce, but he could not walk. He looked around for a dagger or a sword, something sharp with an edge to cut the ropes, but there was none.

Frustrated and resigned, he laid back down on his back and stared up at the sky in the darkness.

As he cried deep tears, the wound inside of him surfaced. Inside of him came a lie and a covenant. Inside was the agreement of the pain that his past produced. Inside of him was the son, the little boy, that child that said, "I cannot do this for I despise myself. I am nothing and always will be."

The Man rolled to his side and sobbed. His heart was breaking, but here was the revealing sight. His tears stung his eyes, and the piercing echo of the past rang true in his soul. Here was the pain, but what could he do with it?

He rolled onto his back and looked up into the sky. Up until now, he could not see the stars, but now, at last, he could perceive them. The stars sparkled and twinkled and shined in the night. He stared and marveled at them. Could these be the ones of the midnight sky who guided sailors on the high seas? Could these be the ones that determine the destination in darkness?

What marvelous insight they bring! How wonderful that there is a way to walk in the shadows of life. "Amazing," he thought.

He looked out at the night and noticed the patterns and constellations and then he remembered the stories and characters of the constellations. The words of the stars spoke with deep wisdom.

One star burst into bright light. In fact, it was staggering as the incredible pinpoint of light broke through the darkness, the light made a star-cross image and seemed to point down to the horizon, or off into the distance, as if it was a guiding light leading us to a savior.

The Man sat up and saw the sign. A small glimmer of hope rose within him. Something divine was happening. Something special was taking place.

The Man hopped up onto his feet, even though the rope still bound him. The Man shouted to the sky, "Help! Can someone help me? I am lost and the travelers have left me alone, robbed, and broke! Help!" Even though there was a sign of hope inside of his heart, he still felt alone.

A small noise came off in the distance behind him. The Man turned around and looked. About a half-mile away there were three camels that rode at a persistent speed, and they were coming toward him. The men on these three camels had lamps that guided their pathway so they would not stumble or fall into a ditch.

More hope rose inside the Man's heart. "Hey! You! Can you see me? Do you know where I am? Help!"

The three camels and their men approached the Man bound by the feet. The Man looked up at these Three. Now, the Three before him wore crowns on their heads and had beards. Robes of satin and purple cloth adorned them. Jewels and gold sparkled on their cloaks. The camels too had rings of gold and silver in their snouts and ears. Here was royalty, and the man knew it. He dropped to his knees and bowed low.

"Arise, my son," said the one closest to him.

The Man stood up and tears filled his eyes. Shame and hope mixed and spun inside his heart; he might meet his death soon.

The king spoke. "You seem lost. What are you doing here in the desert? And where is your camel?"

The Man looked around and saw he was nothing, bankrupt. "I, I don't know. I met the travelers and ate their meat. It was good for a time, and I loved their music, but it was an awful noise. They robbed me of all I have."

The king looked at the Man, shirtless, dirty, broken down, and bound at the feet. And yet he loved him.

The king replied, "But you have your hands. What are you doing with them?"

The Man said, "I have tried and tried to free myself. But I cannot walk. Now I am stuck and am hungry and very thirsty."

The King paused and stepped off his camel. His robe flowed around him and the gold sparkled and glistened in the starlight. The Man couldn't see his face, but a dim glow of blue light came from the King's countenance.

The King pulled out a dagger in a flash. "This won't hurt," he said. And the King stooped down and cut off the ropes between the Man's feet. The Man danced in delight and was free to move around.

The King asked him, "So, my son. Where do you want to go? You have a long journey ahead of you. You might need water. Here, fill yourself up."

The King took from one of his companion's camel a wineskin, but it was empty.

The Man asked, "Where can I get water? This is the desert, there is nothing here."

"You may have been eating bitter meat, my son, but there are in fact, two wells here in the desert. Come with me." And the King led the son out into the valley.

The moon rose off in the horizon and it seemed bigger than normal. Its light poured out over the land of the desert and the King led his son forward. The Two Companions of the King rode their camels and followed them.

In a short distance, the King and the son came to two different wells in the desert. The King dropped a container into one well, and they could hear it fall far below and splash down. The water was very far away. After a moment, the King pulled up the container and produced the water.

"Here," he said as he handed him a drink.

The Man stepped up and drank. The taste was bitter and horrible in his mouth. He spat it out and choked, almost vomiting.

"What!" he said. "How can this be? This is the worst water I have ever tasted. I feel like death has gripped me."

The King threw the container to the ground and walked over to the other well. Again, he took a new container and dropped it down. They heard a splash, as if the water was much closer to the surface. And then the King drew out its water.

He offered it to the son, but the son was cautious, for he felt unsure and unable to trust the King.

"Please, take it," said the King.

The Man stepped forward and took a sip. "Oh my!" he cried out. "Oh my!" he cried. He took another sip, and then another, and yet another. He drank deep of this water. "It tastes so good, so sweet, so wonderful. How could I have ever missed this? How could I ever have missed this water?"

The King said, "My son, there are two wells in my Kingdom. You choose which one to drink. This is my promise to you: if you drink of the sweet well, you will never thirst again. I have come in the middle of the night, to give you back more than you have lost."

With that, the other two companions stepped off their camels and produced a royal robe and a crown with a single jewel in it, and placed it on the Son's head. Then they wrapped the robe around him. Next, they washed the Son's feet and removed his shame and placed beautiful slippers on them, encrusted with jewels.

The generosity of the King overwhelmed the Son. "How could you do this for me? Why?"

The King replied, "But every day with me is Christmas. You saw my star in the night sky, didn't you? But you heard me come from behind you. I have hemmed you in and you are mine."

The King took his Son's face into his hands and drew him close. The King smiled big and laughed. Delight was all over his face and he kissed his Son on the forehead.

"Stay away from the travelers," he whispered.

And with that, the King, his Two Companions, and their camels vanished before his eyes. The Son still held the container of the sweet well and he drank more. Love and life filled him, and he continued to drink. In fact, it was such sweetness that joy flooded his soul, and soon he fell asleep.

That night the Son slept deep and the dreams that passed through his mind were images of life and hope.

He awoke the next morning to a beautiful sunrise. His camel returned and stood next to him, and a small fire and coals and bread rested next to him. It was breakfast time. He ate his fill and mounted his camel. He looked out at the horizon and saw he was about to leave the valley, and he went on his way again.

This time he carried the sweet water, and no longer drank from the well of bitterness. And from there, he returned to his journey.

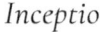

Inceptio

RAIN OF HEAVEN

Strolling in the desert, a lady walked amongst the wildflowers and cacti. Through the red rocks, boulders, and hills, she came through many valleys. For many days she traveled up and over the mountains looking for her heart's desires.

As she walked, she came before a large rock formation of many stones piled on top of each other. She saw rock wall paintings from ancient civilizations that once lived in the land. She examined the petroglyphs. She saw that there were many tales, many stories, and people and adventures that once took place here.

She thought, "I used to think that I was lost, and that there was no place here," but as she peered at the paintings, she saw that the hunts and the wars and the victories were all echoes of the human experience.

For this woman, the woman of delight in the desert is one of the human experience. She knew the nights and days of life. She was dark and beautiful, for the sun and the light of the land caused her smile to shine. But inside her heart was the Journey.

She didn't know where it would take her or what form it would shape before her eyes, but she delighted in herself and in the beauty of the land.

"This Journey," she thought, "would take me many places. I trust the winds and I trust the path before me. Let us walk, for I will know my destination when I arrive. I am satisfied here in the land. Are there no hidden treasures in the burrows, in the desert plants, and the animals here? Is there no life found here in the desert? It is my home and I desire to take root here."

She picked up her belongings and stood before the rocks with the petroglyphs and kissed the rock. "These are my tales as well," she whispered.

Off she went, climbing the red rocks, and looked out high above the desert. She climbed more and more and walked around the boulders and the sitting stones until she reached the top of the small mesa in the desert.

To the west, she could see that the sun would set in a few hours and the shadows stretched out from the tall cacti. To the east, she could see the moon lifting above the horizon. This was the desert moon, and it was a golden yellow light in the late of the evening.

Both heavenly beings surrounded her, where the day started and where the day ended. Not only was heaven before her and after her, but heaven was also above.

To the north came the clouds, some thunderheads that flowed off the mountains and down into the valley. The smell of the desert changed, as there was moisture in the air.

She stepped down off the rocks and made her way to higher ground, where any flash floods may not block her rescue. She soon found her way and went back through the valley again as the rain clouds built and a deep blue and purple thunderhead flashed some lightning.

Up and out of the valley she came and found some old, ancient adobe houses that rested in the cliffs on the high rock walls.

Thunder clapped off in the distance and the rain began. But there was something new here in the atmosphere. This wasn't a rain of destruction or pain, but a rain of delight; for this was the Rain of Heaven.

The raindrops sprinkled and speckled the ground, and the plants grew. The yucca grew taller and wider, the cacti burst with flowers, pink and yellow blossoms that brought new life to the land.

Here, even the desert animals came out of their caves and their holes in the ground and seemed to dance, sing or spin around in the rain.

This, too, caused the Lady to come out of her home in the desert and dance in the heavenly atmosphere. She leaped, spun, and delighted in the rain. It was such a joy that she lifted her face to the heavens and the rains came down.

After a moment of joy, she looked down and saw that the rain which fell on her body became jewels of many colors, and that gold wove in her hair. She realized that out of this heavenly rain were treasures from above.

She marveled as it covered her skin and her clothes and adorned her with riches. The animals also stopped their dancing and came to her and bowed before her as the rain stilled above them.

They seemed to address her with their singing and even a desert owl came and perched and hooted, "Who? Who? Who are you? Who are you but the Queen of the Desert?"

The Queen of the Desert saw her court's guests in front of her and she bowed low. She said, "With delight and honor, I address you. You have been here with me when even I didn't know where I was going. But you have surrounded me with pleasure despite the harsh sun. Now I honor you for the hidden things you bring me."

The desert coyote came before her, and in his mouth was a

golden dagger. He placed it at her feet and spoke, "This tool is not a weapon of death or destruction, but one to cut open the fruit of the land and draw out its nourishment. You have eyes that can see the fruit of the desert in others and bring out its nourishment. You walked lost before here, but now we found you. You, too, can bring about nourishment from the desert."

Next, a wild jackrabbit with tall ears hopped before the Queen of the Desert. In its mouth was a cork from a bottle with a screw in it. "Here, my lady, this is for you. You can open up new wine and plug the pain in the people. As you release the new wine, you bring healing to them. And then you can stop the pain and it will disappear. You know the seasons of the spirit better than others. You can tell when the clouds and the winds are shifting far off in the distant lands. This allows you to witness the new wine forming in the place where you are. Now please, bring out the new wine and let us drink and be satisfied!"

A little lizard waddled up onto a rock and faced the Queen of the Desert. In his mouth was a tiny, golden key. The Queen opened her hand and the little lizard dropped it. He spoke, "You have the freedom to open up new treasures in the people's hearts, even things that others may think are insignificant. You have freedom to release, and freedom to give. Freely you have received, therefore freely go."

And with that, the rain began pouring again and there was a dance in the desert. The Queen flowed and spun around and blessed all the animals of the wilderness. She has found her home and the people she will meet, she will bless.

The rain washed away the refuse, and the pain in her heart soon went away. The sunset and the colors were beautiful. A smile came across her face and gold seemed to drip down on her cheeks. These were not tears of sorrow but treasures of delight, for the Rain of Heaven came.

Inceptio

THREE YOUNG GIRLS

It was a glorious and sunny day in a field of wildflowers in the Rocky Mountain countryside. Three beautiful young girls; three princesses, in fact, ran through the tall grass as they held their hands out to feel the flowers as they flew by.

They picked the colorful wildflowers, made crowns for their hair and they sniffed the sweet aroma of the daisies, lupines, and penstemons.

The clouds were puffs of pillows in the air as the sun glowed in the deep blue sky. Looking up, Hannah saw something flying with great speed and elegance. "Look!" She cried.

Katie and Maddie turned their heads up to the sky. This "something" was gaining great speed. It looked like a flame of lightning shining with all the colors of the rainbow coming right at them! Flowing fabric and streams whispered in the wind like wings coming from its back. It shone as if it were the sun and stopped about thirty feet in the air above and stood before them.

The appearance concerned Maddie, as she was afraid. This being was beautiful and looked down upon them. Katie stood up and stepped forward. "Who are you? What do you want?"

"I am the Lady of the Wind!" Her voice sounded like many rushing waters as her words rippled through the three princesses' hearts. Her sound penetrated their soul. It was frightening, but comforting.

"The voice of the King has called me to you. Come up here!" Maddie, Katie, and Hannah felt light as they floated up to the Lady of the Wind.

As they drew closer, they could see more of her hair and clothing. Silver threads and jewels adorned the border of her white cloak in a great pattern. Flowing strips of white cloth made beautiful patterns with swirls and waves on them. It looked as if even the wind attached itself to her body.

Another thing they noticed was that she smelled so fresh and clean, beautiful, like the flowers in the field they were just in.

Maddie, Katie, and Hannah's eyes grew large as the Lady of the Wind brought them to her.

"Do not be afraid, my children. I have come at the beckoning of the Voice of the King. He has asked me to show you some things that only you shall see. He needs you and desires you to come with me. Will you do just that? Will you come? Will you let me show you great things?"

Maddie, Katie, and Hannah looked at each other in awe. They thought about this request. As they looked at each other, they just knew that everything would be fine. Katie answered, "Take us where you like! We want to see this."

Snap! The wind blew, and they all flew at incredible speed over the valleys and the mountains of the land they lived in. The wind was cool and colorful as streams blew past the Lady of the Wind. Colors like the rainbow flew past them, trailing behind them off into the distance.

Somehow, all three young princesses held close to the Lady of the Wind. She took them higher and higher, the air becoming thinner and cold. They almost couldn't breathe. Maddie choked and gasped for air.

The Lady of the Wind stopped flying, and they floated high above the land, five miles or more.

The Lady of the Wind spoke. "Take the flowers in your hair and breathe into them. They will provide all the oxygen you need. Rest for I will now show you something grand."

The three beautiful young princesses grabbed the flowers from their hair and took a deep breath. They felt better, and no longer felt scared. Hannah grew some courage and asked, "Why are we here? What is going on?"

The Lady of the Wind pointed to the Earth below. "This is your land, this is your country. Do you see all the clouds and the storms of the air below? Some are here and some are there, but there are some areas with no storms and the sun shines, correct?"

Maddie answered, "Of course! The rain comes, and the rain goes, but how I love a sunny day."

"Excellent Princess Maddie, and so too, do the storms of the Spirit come and go. The enemy comes in like a storm and wishes to tear apart your cities and your homes. Watch!"

Like an invisible cloth, at the command of the Lady of the Wind, a layer of air tore away from the clouds below them, and now they saw the spiritual weather. It was like a map. Areas of green, yellow, and red shown above the cities as it tried to tear the people apart. Flashes of lightning blasted below. They heard claps of thunder and pops and crackles as if there was a battle raging below them.

Other beings similar to the Lady of the Wind flew in and out, up and down, chasing globs of dark, evil smoke. Cries of terror came out of these beasts, which were the enemy.

Katie cried, "What is that? Why are they fighting?"

"That is the enemy, Princess Katie. A battle is at hand and the King needs the three of you. Some of us fight and war, but we need 'Your Words'. Your words must speak out and breathe life into us. Although we are great and mighty, full of splendor and power, your words give us what we need to speak to the enemy and destroy their plans."

"I am giving you this map," she said and the Lady of the Wind snapped her fingers. In an instant the huge map of the green blobs of spiritual storms folded up and became small, flying into the hand of the Lady of the Wind. It became like a small envelope. The Lady of the Wind handed it to Maddie.

"My child, take this map. Open it when you need to see where the storms are and where the storms plan to go, and then speak what the Voice of the King says to you and you will give life to us as we fight the battles for you."

Maddie took the envelope, which looked white and ordinary, but she knew inside was a great strategy. She felt privileged that the Lady of the Wind gave this to her.

"I will wait and listen for His Voice," Maddie said, "But, how will I know when he speaks?"

"His voice is deep inside your heart. He knows your fears, and he knows your needs. His voice is familiar and close, like a true Father of the Heart. Listen to him and do what he says and you will have great success. Now come, there is more."

Whoosh! In another flash, they left the great space in the sky and found that they were riding on horses running in a great field.

Hannah held on tight to her horse, a great white steed, as they raced toward the horizon. Gold and silver flowers adorned her bridle. Katie pulled ahead of her on her horse, a beautiful and tall mare with brown and white spots. Diamonds and rubies adorned her bridle. Maddie pulled alongside with her horse, a powerful black stallion. Maddie's bridle was white and emeralds adorned it as she held on tight.

The Lady of the Wind flew above them and commanded the Princesses to steer to the right and left. Back and forth they raced as they reached the edge of the Grand Canyon.

As soon as they came to the edge, they stopped and looked out at the view. Before them was the Canyon, layered with red and orange rock as the sunset. Far below them was the Colorado River, flowing with dark emerald green waters.

The Lady of the Wind hovered before them. "Inside your hands are the bridles of the great steeds you sit upon. Let the Voice of the King steer you and guide you as you ride across the land. These steeds will go wherever you want, over any mountain and through any valley. Listen to the Voice, and you will find the way."

It amazed Maddie, Katie, and Hannah! Their steeds moved to the left and right at their command. Inside their hearts, they knew they could ride them with confidence and that they could hear the Voice of the King and go wherever they needed.

Then the Lady of the Wind flew in front of each of them and handed them a quill: a beautiful, feathered pen. Hannah's was white, Katie's was blue, and Maddie's was red. "These are your quills, the pens of the Voice of the King. Soon days will come when you dream His dreams and you will hear His Voice. When he speaks, write what he says, and you will know the mysteries of the Spirit. If he gives you a dream, be sure to record it with your quill so it will not escape you. Take care of these, for the words and images you receive will be precious and valuable. You will see things and know things. And just like the bridles for the great steeds you ride, they are important so treat them with utmost care. And be careful about those whom you share what His Voice speaks. He will tell you with whom to talk to and when. What to say and what not to say. Guard these words in your heart and treasure them. Be careful with whom you share because they could steal them away. Rest in this, and you will see how to speak. Don't be afraid when he says it is good to speak. You can do this, I am sure."

The three beautiful princesses, Maddie, Katie, and Hannah, took the quills in their hands. As soon as they touched the quills to paper, they heard the sounds of running water in their hearts. It sounded like streams in the mountains, or waves crashing on the ocean's beaches. Inside their hearts were a wind and a breath, still, but always moving and ever guiding.

Suddenly, He spoke! "Follow me, and I will guide you along the path. I will take care of you and make you safe. Now! Go! Take your hearts to the horizon and be with me."

The three beautiful princesses kicked at their steeds, and the mighty horses galloped off the edge of the Grand Canyon, only to fly into the air, higher and higher. The sun sank below the horizon and it was glowing deep orange and red colors. The three beautiful princesses rode hard into the starry night and went wherever the Voice of the King guided them.

Inceptio

AVALON

The battlefield was quiet and still soaked in blood. Countless bodies of knights, soldiers, and pawns of war littered the ground. Smoke rose into the air, and the scavenger birds hovered above, looking for their next feast.

Throughout the array of the dead, some could hear groans from the wounded and dying. It was a great battle and none but few remained to tell of its tale. And yet in the center of the field laid dead the Great Dragon Obsolom. This beast was the enemy of the land.

Hundreds of arrows pierced the dragon's body. Dozens of swords tried their might against the fiery animal. But these wounds and attempts did nothing to bring down the Great Dragon.

The only thing that remained to defeat the beast was to strike the eardrum of the dragon, the softest spot in its body. His head lay down on the ground and his tongue hung between his large, sharp teeth. Obsolom was dead and the soldier John the Mighty had discovered his weakness and won, but it looked like the victor had also become the victim.

Something stirred on the ground underneath the head of Obsolom. Someone was still alive! Miraculously John the Mighty moved his legs, which the head of the dragon had crushed with its weight.

John thought they lost all during his fight with the devilish dragon. He was among hundreds of fellow soldiers doing their best to remove Obsolom from the country. The dragon vented his fiery breath across the homes and tormented the people. Over and over fields of grain burned and precious livestock died under the plague of the land. Obsolom was a true curse, and John and his team vowed to defeat him.

With the remaining bit of his strength, John lifted the head of the dragon and crawled out from underneath the body. He sat up and saw his sword named Marcurleon still punctured the head of Obsolom. With a closer look — to his despair — he saw that the fight broke Marcurleon into two pieces. His hand was still frozen to the handle of his sword, and its blade showed a jagged, shattered end.

He cried out, for Marcurleon was his treasure, his inheritance from his father. The sword Marcurleon was an epic weapon he used in many, many battles. There were huge fights and wars he saw and the sword could tell many tales of last-minute strategies and difficult victories, but it was his trusted weapon, and now the battle of death upon the field of Obsolom marked the end of an era for John the Mighty. Or — so he thought.

John stood up and found himself with a wound in his right leg and he limped his way around the head of the Dragon. He took his dagger from his sheath and cut the throat of Obsolom, deep, to make certain the beast was dead. Dark blood oozed out, and he saw that beast had been dead for many hours. At last, there was no more life in him.

John the Mighty tore a piece of clothing off a soldier's body and wrapped it around the stuck piece of Marcurleon. He pulled and groaned, and the shattered sword came out of the dragon's eardrum.

Caws and cackles of crows and birds of prey gathered around and circled above in the sky in even more numbers. The scavengers then dove and the great feast began. The sound was horrific. John gathered his senses and folded the two pieces of Marcurleon in the cloth, and he hobbled his way off the battlefield.

At the edge of the forest, off in the distance, stood John's horse named Shining. He had a beautiful white coat and was still full of life and excitement as his master walked up to him.

"Come, my blessed steed. You have saved me once again in battle. I knew you'd never leave me."

John pulled himself up and mounted Shining and placed the pieces of Marcurleon in the saddlebag. Together, they rode their way from the battlefield and into the forest.

The sun was still up and there were two to three hours of light left. Surprised, John found no survivors on the field and he marveled that he, in fact, was the only one. The battle was so huge and terrible that nothing in Obsolom's way seemed to stay alive.

As Shining galloped his way down the road, the pain in John's leg grew more intense and he noticed that some blood trickled down the steed's white body. Somewhere he was still bleeding from his wound, and his head felt faint.

John knew that if he could only make his way to the edge of the ocean and return to its shore, he could find the help he needed and a way home. But Shining's gallop became more intense and the trees that blazed by made John's vision dizzier. He became more and more light-headed and soon he slumped on the horse's neck and held on for dear life. And in a moment he passed out.

Sometime later John the Mighty felt cool water on his face. He was lying on the ground and the waters of a lake lapped up and touched him. He stirred, going in and out of consciousness.

Glowing light grew bright around him and somehow his body lifted in the air and someone laid his body in a boat. John moaned in pain, "Where am I? Somebody... help."

Time passed and John lay on a stone slab. His wounds were wrapped in cloth. His body was cleansed from all impurities. Rest came and he lay deep in sleep. No dreams found him, neither did nightmares. It was as if he was in a void and heavenly beings around him repaired his body and soul. The sounds of battle were behind him, and silence surrounded him once again.

John's eyes blinked. He opened them and sat up. He sat on a wooden bed with a warm blanket that covered him. He was inside a small cottage, and the fireplace in front of him cooked a small pot that piped the chimney with its steam.

Peace filled his being, and the aroma of the place smelled of sweet cinnamon and honey. He got up and saw that someone clothed him with a new shirt and pants. All was well. He opened the pot, lifted a small spoon, and tasted the confection. Oh, it was such a sweet taste and delight.

"Where am I?" he asked aloud.

John walked to the door and opened it. Outside were a series of many trees, and the grass on the ground was cut short and groomed to perfection. It seemed more than real. Everything was in order and the place felt like heaven on earth. Restoration was here. John felt alive.

He walked around and looked at the unique forest. Birds chirped, the wind blew, and the branches eased in the top of the trees.

"Welcome," said a small, beautiful voice behind John. He turned around and saw a tall woman with short white hair dressed in a silver, sheer gown. She was beautiful, elegant, and her smile was delightful and marvelous. The lady stepped forward and bowed in front of him.

"Please, there is no need," he said with his hand held up. The beautiful woman stood up and looked into John's eyes. Her sight caused his breath to become short. He asked, "Who are you?"

"I am Avalon. This is my island, my place of healing."

Amazed, John looked around further into the trees that surrounded the cottage. He moved out and saw that a huge body of water circled the area. Only off in the far distance and through the fog could he see the shore.

"How did I come here? How have you healed me?"

Avalon's voice spoke, and this time her words sounded like rushing waters. "Your horse Shining called out to me and brought you here. Your wounds were too great, and they almost got the best of you. My island is the source of your restoration. I have mended your injuries and called life back into you."

John felt his body with his hands. He looked down at his skin. "My scars! My scars! Even they are gone! How did you do this?"

"I am the one to take you from battle and bring you back to it once again. Your time here is sure, but short, for the people still need you. Your time of fighting isn't over, but for the war that is ahead of you, you've needed life to return to you again."

John's eyes were wide open. He looked at the woman, Avalon, and thought how beautiful she was. "You seem... so familiar to me. I must know you from somewhere. Have we met before?"

"I come in various forms, dear John the Mighty. What you see of me now is like the person closest to your heart." Avalon smiled and took John's hand and led him away from the cottage. Together they walked to a small stone reflection pond that stood above the ground and was about four feet in diameter. Glowing light shined out of it, and the waters seemed to spin and flutter.

"Look and see," said Avalon.

John gazed into the waters and there an image appeared of a beautiful woman and her young son. The woman looked just like Avalon, but she was more tired and worn. The woman in the vision worked hard in a field of dirt, plowing and sowing seed. It was a difficult labor, and the baby cried and called out for his mother. Day after day the woman plowed and tilled the soil, but over time the ground loosened and soon the rains came and little sprouts of plants grew out.

Avalon spoke. "John, here is your delight. Here is your field of labor. Together you both have overcome many, many trying times. Here is her battlefield. And now you see you both can work together, though the forms of warfare look different."

John shook his head. "But no! My battles are over! My sword Marcurleon is broken. The Great Dragon Obsolom snapped it in two. I have failed. My father passed that sword down to me from all my generations. I have lost it."

Avalon took John's hand again and led him away from the pool of light. The memory of his broken sword grieved him and he walked in a daze, as though he didn't know where to go with his life.

Avalon then brought him into a garden where many vines and their branches draped over white lattices and arches. In the center of the garden of vines stood a tree stump. It was about three feet in diameter and branches sprouted out from its base, for even though the tree that once stood there was gone, the root was still alive.

In the center of the stump stood his sword Marcurleon, whole, shining, bright and new. Its point stuck into the wood deep down. Lights of energy and life flowed up and out of the stump and entered the metal of the blade. The handle of Marcurleon pulsed in glowing light and changed colors with each moment of intensity.

John's eyes grew large once more. He then ran up to the stump and pulled out Marcurleon. The energy flowed out of the sword and entered his arms and body as he turned it over and examined it.

"This... This is amazing! How did it happen?"

"The tree trunk here is your destiny. The great battle with the dragon tried to cut off your purpose. But as you can see, it is too great and full of life, that nothing will stop the inheritance you carry. I, Avalon, have mended your sword. Your weapon, your tool and your craft are now even stronger than before." Avalon paused and then asked him, "Now tell me something... What was it that enabled you to defeat Obsolom?"

John held Marcurleon and felt the blade with his hand as he remembered the battle. "I struck the Dragon in the eardrum. Marcurleon pierced his brain and he died."

"Yes, for it is your true sound that defeats the dragon. Your weapon sings now if you can hear it," smiled Avalon. "Go ahead, try. Be quiet and listen to Marcurleon."

John lifted the blade to his ear and took a deep breath and listened. At first, there seemed to be a whispering hum from the sword. But the sound grew louder and then notes of harmonics vibrated out and pulses of music resounded. Then came a wonderful melody, and the sword seemed to shout in delight a song of praise and joy.

John grinned and with a quick motion of his arm he sliced through the air with his singing sword, the New Marcurleon. With each stroke, a beautiful cascade of notes fluttered out. He moved his feet forward and pivoted on them and turned his arms and tried out different exercises. The sounds amazed John. It was a symphony of might and a song of power. The more he moved, the louder the notes became. He was the conductor of his own orchestra, and his baton was his weapon of choice.

"This is awesome!" he exclaimed. John stopped moving the sword and held it vertically in front of his eyes. He stared at the humming New Marcurleon.

Avalon stepped before John the Mighty and touched the edge of the singing sword. "You carry a greater weapon. You are stronger now more than ever and it is your new sound that will free the world from destruction. You have seen the battles. You have seen the fallen and the darkness of it. You have hidden in the shadows, but now I call you forward into the light. No longer will you follow another, but today I give you the rank of general of the land. Today is your new promotion. Oh, you thought you had seen the best of the battles, but I call you up higher even now, into the new forefront of your destiny. I am Avalon, your promoter."

John stared at the blade that shined in front of him. And after a moment he turned the New Marcurleon down and placed it into his scabbard. Then he faced the woman.

"Thank you, Avalon. Your words... they've healed me. Your form reminds me of home. I will return to her with love anew. My son needs me. My wife needs me. You are the image of my delight. I hope to meet you again when I need you."

Avalon smiled and looked down to the ground. "Ah, I cannot appear to you this way again. I will come, yes, but in another form. But for now... return to the one who loves you. She longs for your heart and sings for you once again. Show her your new weapon. For the New Marcurleon will sing a new song for her and that will heal her heart. She knows you are a warrior and that you belong not only in the home but also on the battlefield. Her words to heaven have saved you many times over and together you both shall sing new songs again. Fear not John the Mighty. Your promotion is now here."

And at the end of her breath John looked up at Avalon and her body shimmered in the light and in an array of dazzling spectacles she dissolved away in the wind. Next, the surroundings of the island smeared and glowed with life. Gusts of air blew and leaves and branches picked up into the sky, and John looked out as a new tempest howled around him.

The Island of Avalon flew away and John's eyes closed shut, as it was too intense to look. Pieces of the island continued to blow into his face, and he stood strong. And then the wind calmed, and he looked, opening his eyes.

There John stood in the fields of his farm and saw his home with his horse Shining standing next to it. In the doorway was his delight, and she carried his son in her arms. The fields were full of crops and the plants were green and in bloom. John sprinted and ran up to the woman and kissed her on the mouth. He smiled, "I'm home! I'm home! I am no longer alone on the battlefield. Thank you for everything. Thank you. I owe you my life."

And so he kissed her once more and together they entered their house and shut the door behind them. John the Mighty received his healing and soon he was ready to fight again. At last, his inheritance had found its true sound. The New Marcurleon would defeat the next enemy, and his strength was even greater than before.

Inceptio

SKY OF FIRE

It was dark in the middle of the night in the Saharan desert. The dunes ebbed and flowed under the moonlight. The sand ripple and the wind blew across the land. Out here was a man covered with the black cake of the earth. What was once mud, wet and slimy, was now a cracked mask, like a special operations soldier. Here was Jonathan, in the middle of the wild.

He was a warrior, a man of the night, and a man of stealth. Here he was again in the desert, seeking a home and a place to rest his soul.

He walked one step at a time with his feet sinking in the desert sand. At night, the temperature dropped, and the cold chilled him to the bone.

Earlier in the day, it was hot and the blazing sun beat down on him as he hid beneath the sands, trying to rest and stay cool. His friends had fallen behind him as they got lost in the desert, for their minds had gone mad in the sun.

Tonight, Jonathan thought he was alone. He walked, stepped up, and stepped forward higher and higher, for he wanted to reach the top of this large dune. As he crested the dune, he noticed something up ahead.

At first, his eyes could not comprehend what he saw. Was it ocean waves collecting in a form before him? He didn't see nor understand as he blinked and rubbed his eyes. Again he looked.

This time he saw a small white cloud of light and vapor that swirled around like a small wild tornado. Again, he didn't see nor understand, but he drew closer.

As he stepped forward, a great, holy fear came upon him. The tornado rippled like waves of water from the bottom, going up, until it stopped spinning and held tight, but the ripples continued.

A voice came from within and said, "Stand here, my son, for you are with me in this place. I have come to you to give you rest amid war and battles."

Jonathan held tight as his breathing stopped. He couldn't stand the power of the voice coming from within the rippling tornado.

"What do you want from me?" he stammered, choking on his breath.

"I want you. I want you to receive from me. Come closer!"

He stepped forward, not from force and control, but from a deep desire within that caused him to yearn and hunger for more. He lifted his legs as it felt like he was walking through water, but his desire broke through and he finally went forward.

Jonathan took more steps and dropped to his knees. Grief took over him and a deep, sobbing cry came from his soul. Tears dropped from his cheeks and love overcame him.

The rippling tornado floated toward him and enveloped him. The surrounding cloud grew brighter and brighter as he heaved and cried.

"I am with you, Jonathan. I am here. Let me take this load off of you."

Jonathan's body felt lighter and seemed to float around. He looked up and saw a face, a most beautiful face, like nothing he had ever seen. The man in front of him smiled, and a hand that floated in a cloud came to his cheek and embraced his face.

"You've hurt for too long, dear son. I am with you."

The glowing blue hand caressed Jonathan's face and left streams of light on his cheeks that seemed to disappear inside of him.

"Now I want you to look forward."

Jonathan raised his head and looked out at the horizon and he saw a golden yellow lion running toward him. His eyes grew wide as the beast charged. It seemed like slow motion, yet he couldn't stop it.

Jonathan stood up, trying to ready himself for the attack, but the lion leaped through the air and jumped right at Jonathan. The lion became spirit then, and when it landed on Jonathan, it wrapped around his body and disappeared.

The experience shocked Jonathan. He couldn't explain why the lion was there for a moment and then gone the next. His hands and arms were still braced for the attack, but he looked around and saw nothing was there. The lion was gone, and so was the cloud or rippling tornado.

He looked up; saw the moon overhead and the stars twinkling in the night. Ahead, in the sky, above the horizon, there seemed to be a pink and purple cloud hovering in the air. It looked like the aurora borealis. It looked like fire in the sky.

From within him, a roar shouted like a lion.

The next thing Jonathan knew was his body flew up into the air as fast as a fighter jet in the dark night and moonlit sky. He whizzed up and around and could see the desert below and the rock formations that dotted the land.

Higher and higher he found himself in the clouds, far up in the atmosphere. He was two or three miles above the floor of the earth. He spun around and flew around the clouds. Something inside of him shouted for joy!

He flew, straightened out, and made a beeline for the moon, which was on the horizon. Up ahead was a large, puffy, bright light-blue cloud. As he got closer, flashes of lightning blasted from within the clouds. And he disappeared from sight as he entered the cloud.

As soon as he was there, Jonathan stood on a mountain within the misty cloud. There were other people here.

Jonathan saw them; they glowed with white light and stood in a long row, standing side by side. He thought he should have fear, but he wasn't afraid. Something curious inside of him desired to meet them. He walked toward them.

The men and women who stood before him smiled as he walked past them in their row. As he walked by them, they followed him. The row of glowing white people looped around and stepped up behind him.

Jonathan didn't notice at first, for he was more curious to look at their faces as they smiled, so he looked deeply into their eyes. But as soon as Jonathan came to the last man he stopped and saw all followed him.

"What? Why are you following me?"

The ones behind him spoke with the voice of rippling ocean waves, "We are the signs that follow you, dear Jonathan."

One of them spoke. "I am a promise, a voice from the past that will become clear in your future. You can count on me. I will be there when you most need me."

"So will I," spoke another. "I am your reward. I am with you." As Jonathan saw these people, he noticed in their hands gold.

Altogether, they held out their hands and opened their palms up. Inside each palm was a small nugget of raw and wild gold. It sparkled bright yellow in their light blue hands. In fact, oil dripped in their hands from the gold and oozed out and flowed to cover their hands.

Jonathan was amazed and desired to know more, but they dissolved away. "I am with you," said their voices as they faded into the cloud. Jonathan turned around and looked at the mountain and its rocks. He noticed that up ahead at the mountain's peak, something bright flashed in a repeated pattern.

He climbed up and saw at the top a very tiny lighthouse, half the height of his body. Its top light spun around and around in a strong and brilliant way. The light coming from the lighthouse showed bright, cutting its way through the mist and the clouds.

"What is this?" he thought to himself. "How can it be so small and so tiny and yet this bright light shines from within it?"

He looked and marveled at it. He rested here for the night and fell asleep at the top of this mountain. He had dreams within dreams. Sometimes, he couldn't tell if he was awake or sleeping. The dreams within dreams disturbed him because there were many things he didn't understand, but he kept dreaming.

Night after night, there were more night visions and sometimes there were some more real than the ones before. People would come to him, people from other countries, even people from other times, from the past and from the future.

All of them told him the Great King sent them to him to speak about his future and how to walk on the path of his life. Knowledge, wisdom, and understanding filled him. His eyesight became clearer and clearer and his ears became sharper and sharper.

New light filled his imagination and solid understanding helped him to speak to the kings and queens of the land.

Farmers of the land also came to him and took from Jonathan seeds of gold from his lips and from his hands. As the farmers planted them, bountiful crops overflowed in the land. The reapers of the fruit of the land overtook those who sow, and soon the people said, "Stop! It is too much! We have more than enough, more than we can ever need!"

The words from Jonathan's mouth shook the mountains of the surrounding land. People saw him and fell down, for they didn't see him, but the lion spirit within. They were afraid, for they knew that he came not just in words, but in demonstration.

Jonathan never forgot the words, "I am with you." For deep inside of him, he saw the face and the hand that embraced his cheek and healed his heart. That vision and that purpose never left him, and thus he could also walk and dance with the rippling tornado cloud that always surrounded him. Some didn't see the cloud, but they knew it was there, for everywhere he went, the atmosphere changed.

Inceptio

THE BEAUTIFUL
FLOWER GIRL

The piles of laundry all over the floor of the laundromat were perfect to dive into and rest in, as any small child could imagine. And this little girl loved to hide from her mom as the days of labor continued to busy the matriarch with an endless list of priorities. The work left little time for them to play with each other and so the girl found other means to find delight.

The little girl hid behind some shirts and spied out, looking to scare her mother. Oh, how she anticipated surprises! Oh, how she loved the surprises of life, for they bring her great joy. "What new thing around the corner would come and kiss me?" she'd ask.

The laundromat was full of people and other children who ran up and down the aisles screaming and laughing. In fact, it was quite a community. Everyone knew each other and would welcome each other's families into their lives. People were open and honest, but their traditions held them down.

The little laundry girl, however, had something special in her hands. The work of her mother was powerful and true, but this little laundry girl could see into the hearts of others and speak love and life. Her imagination was something to behold.

But this ability brought troubles her way because the elders, the people of the community, didn't understand her insights. They said that she should sit in the corner and obey them, do her chores and help cook the food.

She did so, but in her heart, she knew that they didn't understand. For a time, she thought it was her own fault, but after a while, she saw that the others in her life did not see what she saw. They did not perceive.

Her insight into the people grew and matured. No longer was she hiding in the laundry, but now she helped her mother sew and manufacture the clothing in the shops where they worked.

She was beautiful as well. Many men would come to look and wonder about her. However, she knew that within her heart was a great treasure, and she was safe to keep it with her at all times. Many men would hope and desire her, but she knew that there was one for her and her alone.

As time passed, she became a wife and a mother, and people would help her in her crafts, but there was still more inside of her heart. She continued to see and perceive the images of the spirit and the worlds beyond natural sight.

The words and pictures burned within her, and she still yearned for a greater sense of identity. The imaginations of her spirit became her projects of expression, and her craft was her cause.

So she moved forward with her project. However, one day it was her worst. The promised money did not come. The appointments and opportunities fell through, and the people turned their backs on her. Great dishonor came to her, and she sat on the floor crying.

This position reminded her of the days as a child sitting in the laundromat, known as the Little Laundry Girl. Now she was older and more mature, and yet her heart yearned for the days of the community she loved. The past seemed better than the present, and the future proved to have no hope, and she knew that today was no fun at all. This little laundry girl returned to her heart.

As she remembered the past, there was also another story in her. Far away from the city of her youth, there was a small field with some trees she loved to explore. She would lie on her back and look up to watch the clouds in the sky.

The clouds were billowy, white, and fluffy as they drifted. Their shapes revealed characters and animals in her imagination. She would tell herself stories and go on many adventures. These clouds became her friends.

This friendship with imagination was still the problem her beloved community didn't understand. They could not imagine for themselves the hopes and the joys of seeing what was inside the heart.

It was in this field of dreams where she was no longer the little laundry girl, but in fact, in this sanctuary, she became the Beautiful Flower Girl. There was glory in this field, and colors and light sparkled and dotted the green grass.

One by one, she picked little blues, little purples, and little whites and wove them into her hair. It was here that others could see her true beauty, for she had learned to delight in herself.

It was this memory she needed when things went poorly, such as on this terrible day. The money was gone, the promises unfulfilled, and she lost hope. It was this memory that held her together.

Up and off the floor, she rose to walk. There was the decision of movement and hope. She can dream, yes, but she cannot stay there forever. The reality of life is indeed her dream, but out of the dreams come the action and footsteps of fulfillment.

After a few phone calls and emails, she dialed up a close friend and poured out her heart. She cried a little, but her friend listened and brought understanding and joy to her soul once again. This discussion and dialog opened up her heart and helped her see.

Even though she knew how to see into others, it was in her own time of difficulty she needed another to see into her.

A few weeks passed by and the project was gone and the doors were closed. Nothing new was on the horizon, so she resorted to her chores in the house, the work of her hands, and she became the little laundry girl once more.

The dryer was empty and the last wash was in the machine when there was a knock at the door as she folded the clean clothes. For a moment she didn't hear the pounding on her front door, as her thoughts were deep within.

The knocking got louder, and she became aware of the sound. With a rush, she came to the front door and opened the way. Standing in front of her was a postman, and he was quite happy.

"Good news! I found this envelope in my boxes and here it is, the thing you've waited for! I think it's a wonderful surprise!"

The Beautiful Flower Girl's emotions rushed with excitement, and she grabbed the envelope out of his hands and opened it. Inside were a letter and a check from an investor for a large amount of money! The delay was the mistake of several people and all were sorry. The postman was sorry for losing the money. The letter said that they were sorry for the postponement and therefore they had to send the check now!

Life filled the Beautiful Flower Girl's heart, and she saw her project live again. The work of her hands was not in vain, and the people who shut the doors opened them again. The finances continued to come, and soon there was a buzz of activity.

There were those who heard of the Beautiful Flower Girl and because others gave, they wanted to contribute too. Soon everyone came to her and wanted to see what she saw. They wanted to hear what she heard. They desired the heart of her soul, and the surrounding families wanted her to speak and come into their homes.

And as they welcomed her, she told the story about how the field of flowers and seeing those clouds in the sky awakened her imagination and helped her to see again. No longer would she labor in the laundry of life, always cleaning and tumbling, but now her true beauty would open up other's hearts and help them see as well.

Inceptio

GLAMOUR

The woman grabbed her clutch and ran out the door, racing to her taxicab. She was late for her date and she didn't know who she was meeting. Louisa's job faced her with a challenge. She worked hard at her profession and wanted to find the man in charge of the ritzy theater that just opened in the downtown arts district. Its name was The Ascent Auditorium. Her assignment was to report on the various celebrities who planned to show up. But the new owner was a man of mystery. Everyone talked about him, but no one ever saw him. She hoped to feature him in her next article.

Earlier that day, Lousia received a knock on her door with a messenger who handed her an envelope that only had the theater's name on it with a ticket. It said, "See me tonight. I have something to show you. 7 pm sharp."

The problem was, she was late. Just before her time to arrive, she dug through her closet, figuring out what dress to wear and to put on her makeup. Everything was on the line. She had to get this exclusive scoop.

In the taxi, she finished her mascara and took a few deep breaths. Her ride arrived at the destination and dropped her off at the theater's front entrance. The crowd was teeming with excitement, and everyone was looking very nice. Louisa got out her ticket and entered the lobby.

Inside, it was spectacular. The red and the gold ornaments. The lights were perfect. It was a throwback to the golden days of the cinema. Lousia showed her ticket to an usher, and he took her to her seat.

The crowd packed the theater. Everyone was hurrying to finish getting seated as the show was about to start. But the chair next to Louisa on the left was still vacant. Piles and piles of people kept filling the rows of seats, but none came to claim Lousia's empty mate.

She thought to herself, "Maybe he will come and join me."

But the lights dimmed and the orchestra played. The audience buzzed with thrill and excitement. Lousia held her breath. Then the curtain opened. In the center of the stage was a chair and sitting on it was a little boy, about eight years old. He sat with his eyes closed and in his lap were three balls.

The music kicked up, and he started juggling the balls while still in the chair. Louisa looked with curiosity at this opening act. The boy opened his eyes and jumped up, still juggling, and did amazing tricks and maneuvers.

The motion captivated Lousia, and the skill mesmerized her. She thought to herself about all her jobs and her projects and how difficult it was to manage time and energy. And yet this child juggled these balls with absolute perfection. Louisa looked down at her ticket.

"Excuse me. Excuse me. Sorry. Pardon me, my seat is over there."

Louisa looked to her left and saw a man in a tuxedo making his way to the empty chair next to her. She was so excited and happy. She didn't know who this man was.

The man was handsome and sharp-looking. His watch was elegant and the faint but pleasant cologne was pleasing to her senses. She asked, "Is this seat for you?"

The man smiled, and his teeth seemed to sparkle. He showed her his ticket and asked, "J22, correct?"

"Yes, of course."

The man sat down and watched the boy juggle. Louisa couldn't help to wonder if this man was the owner of the theater. Her burning curiosity filled her chest. She had to know.

"Excuse me, sir. Have you ever seen this envelope before?" Louisa pulled out her invitation and showed it to him.

"Why yes. I got one myself. Just today."

"Really!?" Louisa whispered in amazement. "I got this today, too. I am trying to meet the owner of the theater, but no one has ever seen him before. Everyone in the press is dying to meet him. They say he is mysterious and clever."

"Oh? Is that what people are saying? Well, I am looking to meet him soon too. I just wonder where. I work for the ad agency up the street."

Louisa's heart sank. This was a setup, she thought. This was a competitor, a snake. She was sitting with her enemy. Louisa wondered what to do. She was so close to another reporter who might get the scoop before her.

She took a deep breath again and pondered her situation. All she knew from her experiences was to be herself and let her genuine heart shine. She understood she could fake it to make it, but those times never bore as much as fruit as being authentic.

"It's nice to meet you, then."

"The pleasure is all mine. I am Alex."

"Louisa."

The show continued, and her heart grew more anxious. She kept looking around and the performances became more silly. It was a basic tiny kid's vaudeville routine. More acts came out onto the stage.

Lousia excused herself to head to the restroom. As she left, Alex watched her go, and his eyes examined her every move. He smiled and sat back to relax in his chair. At the door, Louisa looked back at Alex. She wasn't so sure about him anymore.

In the bath, Lousia washed her hands and got some air. She paced back and forth. "There must be something else here. Why would I get an invitation and the owner wouldn't show up?"

The lights dimmed in the bathroom and she knew it was the intermission. Lousia hurried back and returned to her seat, and found that Alex was no longer there. The crowd was milling around, and everyone was talking about the show.

Louisa looked around the lobby for any clue. She headed for the box office desk and found a clerk.

"Excuse me. I am looking for the owner of the theater. Can you please direct me to him?"

The clerk was ever so professional and replied, "And who are you to call him?"

"I'm from the newspaper. The State City Presser. He invited me."

"Hmmm. I'm sorry, but he isn't available for interviews today."

"But can you tell me who he is? We've been trying to do a story on him for weeks."

"Sorry, but I am not at liberty to speak to the press. You can call our main office tomorrow."

Frustrated, Louisa fumed and turned around. The clock on the wall ticked, and she looked around, searching. The lights dimmed. The crowd returned to the auditorium.

Lousia watched everyone go in. "Where is that Alex guy? I bet he's already found him."

Louisa went up the stairs, halfway to the balcony. She turned around to look out over the crowd. Nothing. No Alex. Nobody. So she headed up higher and found the balcony rows.

To her surprise, there was a rope, and it cut off access to prevent any seating. It was spacious, empty, and Louisa looked below. The show's second act began and dancers came out. She watched and searched for Alex.

"Excuse me, Louisa?" said a voice behind her.

Louisa turned around and saw the difficult clerk from the box office. He found her.

"He will see you now."

Louisa's heart skipped. Her effort was no longer in vain. She followed the clerk up some steps and went even higher and higher. The clerk led to a wing of sidelights that shined down upon the stage and then some rafters above the ropes and pulleys of the stage that fly in and out the curtains and set pieces. Then the clerk stopped and pointed to a railing that went across the stage but high above, about sixty feet above the show below.

"If you want to see him, go out to the center of the railing and hold tight to the ropes."

Louisa looked and trembled. "What!? Are you crazy? I will fall. I can't go up this high. I am afraid of falling. Are you telling me to be in the center stage? Am I part of the show?"

The clerk smiled. "It is up to your heart's desires. If you want to meet him, you must step out. You can always walk away, can't you?"

And then he left.

The lights were down below and shined hot and bright. Lousia thought she was crazy. She pursued and worked hard, spending countless hours at her job, and now she has the biggest story of her life. It seemed things could end here, or she could take the risk and step out even further.

Lousia looked down and saw how high she was and the stage below. Determined to not give up, she took off her shoes, held them in her mouth by the straps, and moved with care as she stepped out onto the narrow platform. Her hands and arms stretched out, grabbing the ropes as she moved to the center.

Once there, she could look out and see the crowd. They were smiling, but the height terrified her. She asked herself, "How much longer can I do this? I must be crazy. I am even crazier to do this!"

Suddenly the platform moved and the music below changed into a high-energy piece. Louisa freaked as she held on tight to the ropes as the platform sank lower and lower to the stage.

"Oh my God! I am part of the show! I am part of the show! I didn't know this would happen! Holy crap. What will happen next?"

The platform lowered and it exposed Lousia on the stage. The crowd cheered and applauded. Louisa smiled and tried to compose herself as she looked around. The lights changed and the spotlight shined upon her.

Then a voice over the speaker system blasted, "And now would the lady please be willing to step forward onto the stage? Did you receive your invitation?"

Lousia stepped down and slipped on her shoes. She pulled out her invitation. "Here it is!"

The voice said, "Excellent."

The platform raised up and returned to its place above the stage. Lousia looked around.

"What is going on here? I'm not supposed to be part of the show."

Alex then stepped out from the wing onto the stage. "But you are now, my dear."

"You! Alex! Are you the owner?"

The music picked up in a wonderful dance routine. Alex smiled and stepped in front of her, holding his hand.

"Would you be willing to dance with me?"

The request shocked Louisa. Every time she moved forward, there was another invitation, an opportunity that asked of her. But she had to choose. It was her life, her choice, her voice, her actions. Would she have the courage to see where things go?

Lousia took his hand and the dance began. The music sounded wonderful, and they spun around. Alex led, but the grace came from Lousia. Her skill and balance were in perfect order. Her elegance and style let the whole show shine. The crowd went wild. Their eyes fixed on her and Louisa relaxed in the performance. Soon she was gliding back and forth on the stage. Her freedom even impressed Alex. With each twist and spin and every step, she gained more confidence. The dance was memorable and became passionate. Life and energy filled her. The more she danced, the more desire came into her. The music matched her desires and Alex thought he was leading her, but the focus was on Louisa. Everyone in the crowd saw her shine.

The music ended at the moment Alex dipped Lousia down. He picked her up and took a bow, and then gestured to his dance partner. Lousia was out of breath but amazed. The whole routine surprised her as the entire crowd jumped to their feet, cheering her on. Louisa, humbled, smiled, and did a little, curtsied and bowed.

Alex took her off the stage, but she pulled his arm with a fire in her eyes. "Just who are you? Why did you do all of this? You said you work for the ad agency down the street. Are you trying to make fun of me? Make me a show?"

"Didn't you have fun out there? You surprised even me! And yes, I work for the ad agency because I own it. Like I own many businesses."

Louisa looked at him with sudden suspicion. "Other businesses? Like what?"

"Like this theater. Did you enjoy it? The show?"

Louisa's eyes grew enormous with surprise. "You! You're the owner!? Your name is Alex, right? Oh my God! I had no idea."

Alex smiled with striking confidence. Louisa was trying to figure everything out in her mind. She looked up at him with caution.

"But why did you do all this for me?"

Alex looked down at her with loving, kind eyes. "I wanted to see if you were in the business for yourself or not. I know you wanted the scoop. But I had to test you to see if you had the courage and perseverance and not lose your cool. You could have given up at any point. But let me ask you a question. What happened in the dance?"

Louisa looked down in thought for a moment. "I just came alive. I was doing what I saw in my dreams. I found my passion, my life."

Alex replied, "And that's where you belong."

Alex lifted Louisa's hand to his lips and gave it a small kiss. "May you be in that place all the time. You always have the invitation here." He took her hand and placed it onto her chest.

"Never forget the desires of your heart."

Louisa found her cab again and stepped inside. The crowd on

the street gathered around the vehicle, thrilled to see her go. They waved with full excitement. She sat back in her seat and wondered about all the evening's events and moments. It was too much to think through. She put her hand to her chin and looked out the window. The neon lights reflected on the window as they drove by. Awe and wonder filled her eyes.

Louisa said, "It looks like I found my scoop."

Inceptio

THE CASE OF THE MISSING JEWEL

O nce upon a time, there was a clockmaker named Bob who was a master at his craft. He enjoyed everything he did in his shop, even though there were many challenges. He was the inheritor of the business and he worked countless hours, starting early in the morning and late into the night.

Today various collectors sold him many boxes of clocks. Some were in various conditions and they needed repair and work before he could put them on display. His clocks were of different styles and many were quite expensive. They came into his possession after much negotiation. Bob repaired all the clocks, made them well, and put them out for everyone to see.

The public loved them and enjoyed their colors and designs. Their sounds of the tick-tock ticking and the gears turning delighted everyone, for they made magical music. As the people watched them pass their time by, they enjoyed the experience. Bob smiled with glee, and all of his hard work seemed to pay off.

Yet there was one clock he could not fix. He had much trouble with it, as it was a unique cuckoo clock. In the past, it made incredible sounds, and the people loved it so much that they spent countless hours watching the time pass by. But now many critics said, "This clock is too old and doesn't work today. Its time has passed. There is no future for it." Frustrated, Bob hired an assistant who promised him he would find the solution to make this crazy cuckoo clock finally work.

The assistant worked hard and got lots of help from a variety of people. This seemed to make matters worse and confused everyone. No one seemed to have any answers. Bob regretted purchasing the clock and wondered if he should shelve it away. His frustration reached its height. So, after many hours and days of work with the assistant and no solution, the assistant went away. No one had hoped to repair this clock.

Bob said to himself, "Time is money, and money is time. All of these other clocks have produced a profit but not this cuckoo clock. What can I do?"

Bob pulled himself together and made hot tea. He sat down on the end of the couch and looked through an old magazine that featured photos of this clock. He pondered and pondered and soon fell asleep. He began to dream.

In his thoughts, colors came, and he saw new vistas and mountains. He heard birds chirping and songs were singing from mysterious directions. He walked along a path. As he hiked through the mountains, he came up high and looked out over the valley. As he peered, he heard a new sound, a cuckoo sound. "Strange," thought Bob. "Why do I hear this peculiar bird sound? This cuckoo sound doesn't belong in this land."

Bob turned around and saw the source of the sound. The bird was alive and yet made of wood. It sat on a tree branch and continued to make its crazy sound. Next, the bird hopped over to the side and came to a nest. Inside was a single egg that glowed a slight blue and it had speckles on it.

Bob said, "This is incredible! A single live egg from this cuckoo bird? Where has it been all this time? I must see it and take care of it. Perhaps this new birth will enable me to fix the clock!"

And just as Bob walked over to peer at the egg and he reached to touch it, he suddenly awoke!

Bob was still on the couch, and the light was still on. His teacup was empty, and he looked around. "How do I find this egg?" He thought.

An impression came to him. "I know. Where is that old box that the clock came in? Perhaps the old address on the label will give me a clue."

In a rush, Bob got up and went to his storage shed and found the box. On the label, it said, "From: Sight, Sound and Pictures, Inc. To: The Lovers and Dreamers."

It alarmed Bob. "That is not the usual address for a shipping label. Oh well, there must be something more here." So, Bob opened the box and found old dust and it made him sneeze. He felt reluctant, for the smell of the old clock was present and he thought maybe he was just fooling himself. "It's only a dream. But that egg. Hmm."

Bob peered further and lifted some of the inner cardboard flaps and he saw something. Inside was a gear with a blue jewel inset into it. It was the same soothing color as the egg in his dream. "What in the world is this?!" he exclaimed. "This box has a missing jewel in it!"

He carefully picked it up and looked it over with his eyeglasses. In a rush, he took the gear with its jewel and went to the old broken clock. He turned it over and opened it up. Inside he could see that there was much work done, but at the heart of the gears was an opening. Bob took the gear with the jewel in it and placed it in the space. It was a perfect fit!

Bob exclaimed, "Can it be!? Can it finally work?"

The blue jewel in the gear came alive and shone a bright light. The gears started working and turned and turned. The clock made wonderful sounds and even the cuckoo bird chimed. The life returning to the device amazed Bob.

Bob madly worked all night, making slight adjustments. He oiled the gears, making sure all the parts were in order. He felt like a child on Christmas morning. He couldn't contain himself. He knew he could put it on display.

Bob bought many ads in newspapers and word spread throughout the city that Bob's crazy cuckoo clock was working. They all wanted to see it. Even the naysayers and critics were itching to find out and they hoped against hope that something good would happen.

The crowd gathered around Bob's clock shop and waited. Inside, Bob held onto his glee and opened the door. He produced the crazy cuckoo clock for all to see and hear its sound.

The crowd cheered and celebrated. The clock amazed them. They exclaimed, "It sounds like what we remember it used to be, but now it's even better. There is something new about it. Its sound is meant for today."

The event satisfied Bob, and he was eager to show off the clock. The people fell back in love with the timepiece and grew to love it more and more. In fact, the clock became so popular for a season that it was the top clock on display. Bob couldn't be happier.

Later on, Bob found his old assistant and came to him. They

both agreed that at the time each of them did what they could do and they made amends. They were no longer bitter or sad. They solved the problem.

Bob said to himself, "The dream of the egg saved everything. I am totally amazed for I had given up hope."

Bob sat down once more on the couch with his hot tea in hand. He filled himself up and fell asleep yet again. This time his dreams increased, and he saw more lands and more special places and found himself on even greater adventures.

Inceptio

HALFWAY THERE

Kylie walked down the street to the playground and held her hand in her dad's. They continued through the neighborhood and passed many houses. Kylie asked, "Want to go down the slide with me?"

"Sure," said Dad.

"Want to push me in the swing too, Dad?"

"Of course. Do you want me to make you fly to the moon? I can push you really hard."

"No, Dad! I want to go to Saturn. It's my favorite planet, you know."

Dad just smiled, and they arrived at the playground. Tons of kids were there, and the activity was quite intense. All the children were running around and having such a great time. They loved every minute, every second of play.

"Dad! Dad! Look at me! Do you see me? Do you think I am the most amazing astronaut?"

Kylie was up high at the tower of the playground's castle. She popped her head out of the circle window and smiled. She was so happy.

"Kylie, you are an amazing astronaut."

She hopped up and down and headed for the slide. She was a bit too fast, and she suddenly slipped on a piece of the metal slide and fell. She went headfirst down the slide. She cried out for help!

"Ahhh, help!"

Dad ran as fast as he could and caught her on the slide, picked her up, and held her in his arms. She cried badly. Dad rocked her in his arms to calm her down.

"My arm, Dad! My arm!"

Dad carried her to a park bench and looked her over. Her arm had a road burn rash on it because she fell and rubbed against the slide's metal. It was bright red. Dad quickly grabbed his water bottle and poured the cold liquid onto it. Kylie grabbed a hold tighter onto her Dad.

"Ohhhh...."

"It's ok, little one. You just had a nasty fall. It's ok."

Kylie stopped crying and held onto her father. Dad continued to rock and cradle her. It got quiet for a moment.

"Dad, do you still think I can be a great astronaut and get to Saturn? I want to build a house on its rings and live there forever."

"Yes, Kylie, you can do whatever you wish, whatever you want. I will support you."

Kylie looked up into her father's eyes. She still had big teardrops in them.

"Will you come with me to Saturn? I want to make you a cake for your birthday there. We can see all the stars and talk to the aliens. They can have cake too."

"Of course, I'll come! I'd love to have cake... with aliens."

Kylie smiled and got her energy back.

"Let's go on the swing, Dad! You can push me to Saturn!"

Kylie was now feeling much better. They got up and ran to the swing set. But all the kids were using them. They had to wait. Kylie was not happy.

"Dad, we missed the launch again! We have to wait until Saturday." She looked up to the sky and squinted her eyes. "I think the weather delayed us."

But just at that moment, another mom across the way called for her kids on the swing set. Two little girls immediately swung up high and jumped off. They flew through the air and landed on the sand.

Kylie squealed in delight and ran to take an empty seat. Dad ran too and got into position. Kylie kicked her legs and tried to get started, but couldn't make a move.

"Dad! Push me! Push me to Saturn!
It's countdown time! 10 - 9 - 8 - 7 - 6."

Dad started to push. "No, Dad! Too soon!" He stopped.
"5 - 4 - 3 - 2 - 1. Blastoff!"

Dad stepped back and gave her a push. Kylie squealed in delight.

"Weeee! Dad! We're going to Saturn! I can see the moon. I can see the stars. Are you coming?"

"I'm right behind you!"

Dad stretched out his arms to his side and zipped around like a shape shuttle. He made engine noises with his mouth.

"ShhhhooooooooSShhhhhh!"

Kylie loved it.

"We're gonna make it, Dad!"

Kylie kicked her feet and swung back and forth. Dad pushed here and there and kept the momentum.

"Dad, what is across the Milky Way? How far can we go? All the way?"

"It's many light-years across the Milky Way. It would take a long time to reach the other side."

"Will you go with me? Anywhere?"

"Of course. Anywhere."

Kylie smiled. "Even halfway there?"

"Absolutely."

"But isn't halfway there near the big, black hole at the center? We'd get stuck forever!"

"Kylie, I will protect you from any black hole. We'd be fine."

"Ok. Let's go to Saturn instead. I still have to make your cake for your birthday."

Still swinging, they were having a great time. Kylie kept looking into the sky and saw the faint crescent moon. She got even more energy and kicked even more.

"Booster engines ignite! It's time to go to the moon and then Saturn. Or even halfway there! It's time for my dad's birthday!"

And with one big kick, Kylie swung back and pushed her body out of the swing, just at the moment of the highest point of the swing. She flew through the air and sailed.

Dad's eyes opened up wide, and he ran as fast as he could and miraculously caught Kylie in his arms. Kylie laughed in delight.

"Oh, Kylie! Tell me first before you do that. I don't want to take you to the hospital."

Kylie pouted. "But I thought we were going to Saturn?"

Dad stopped and smiled. "Right. We're going. Right now!"

Dad placed Kylie on the ground and started to run back down the sidewalk. Kylie ran after him. Together they held out their arms like wings and made rocket noises with their mouths.

"ShhhoosshhooooSSssoooosssooooshh!"

In their imagination, they flew up and off the ground and into the sky. Far high into the clouds and above the earth's atmosphere. They passed the moon, passed Mars, passed Jupiter, and then to Saturn.

They sat in a wonderful cute house sitting on the rings of Saturn and had cake with aliens. It was Dad's best birthday ever.

Inceptio

"*We did it together!*"... "*We did it together.*"

INCEPTIO

The marble halls of the Great King's court were empty as I walked out of the Throne Room. I felt both happy and sad at the same time. Today was my commissioning, and I must say goodbye to my children, my students, my warriors.

In my days in the courts of the Great King, I saw many wars and many victories. But a new venture was on my heart and today would be the day for a great journey to the far lands beyond the horizon. It would be a journey to the Land of Dreams.

A new command sprang up from the well of my heart. I returned to my classroom, and I gathered my children, my sons, and my daughters to my feet as I sat before them. I loved them, taught them many things about the Kingdom and saw many changes in their lives. But today I had to tell them "goodbye."

Tears came to their eyes, and I reminded them of the expeditions we shared, and I reminded them of the treasures they found. I also reminded them that soon they would stand before other young children and speak into their lives.

"But you're leaving us?" Hannah cried out. She felt terrible and didn't know if she could sleep that night.

"I am returning and I will come back with more for you," I said, as I tried to comfort them.

They held their chairs tight with their small hands and again knew that this journey wouldn't be too long. But they stood up and gathered around me and laid their hands on my shoulders as I sat, and thus they spoke my future to me:

"You will go and strike down the enemies of Light," said Maddie, the warrior princess.

"I see you walking with Kings and Princes," said Jonathan the lion-hearted.

"And many will know the Great King and become Friends of his Court because of you," said Andrew, the gentle one.

It was now that tears filled my eyes. It was bittersweet and tender at heart. I looked at them and peered into their spirits. I still saw the treasures. But I saw their future. And how good and great and grand it is.

I got on my knees and hugged them and gave them this charge: "Today I give you a new command. I want you to sleep."

The children looked around at each other with quizzical faces. I knew that this new directive made little sense at first. But I expanded my vision.

"I want you to dream. I am going to the land of my dreams now, my home, and my future. You must dream. Dream dreams bigger than you can imagine. Dream dreams bigger than what you could do or accomplish on your own, and then arise and awaken and help others dream. When I return I will listen to the stories *you* wrote. I will listen to the treasures *you* released upon the land. Do not return empty-handed. Do not bury your dreams in the ground, for I have invested in you. Remember to dream. Remember to desire. Listen to the King and agree with him on what he speaks about your dreams. I must go now, so come and release me."

More tears filled my eyes and my heart was broken. The children again all came and embraced me. Evan held up signs he drew out for me to see. They said, "You can do it!"

But soon the emotion changed from tears to joy and the children shouted and spurred me on. Cheers filled the room and the playing began. We hopped, we skipped, and we jumped. We ran around and threw and bounced the rubber balls. Life isn't always serious, now is it?

And after we exhausted ourselves, once we had no more breath, we laid flat on our backs and stared up at the sky. Something like satisfaction filled our hearts. We became quiet and could hear our hearts beat.

"Do you know why I always put 'Inceptio' after I finish your stories, your treasures?" I whispered to them. "It is because this is the beginning and not the end. Many have spoken to your future and your treasure, as though the end is near and they themselves have lost hope. But today I place hope in your hearts and say 'go,' for *you* are the beginning. *You* are the start. I have shared in the authorship of your hearts and I say again 'go and dream,' for this is a new thing today."

Love filled our hearts, and I stood up and gathered my belongings. The children exited and ran out to their families. I then took the scrolls of each of their treasures and locked them in a safe place. I left them the keys to the storehouse and to the treasure chest and left them to grow.

Soon I will return from the Land of Dreams, my home. Soon I will find them alive and strong and grown. How I love them, and how much they love me. I long for the days when they will come and say, "We were like those who dreamed."

Now Go...

ABOUT THE AUTHOR

Jurri Schenck

Jurri Schenck is a creative visionary who inspires those he touches. His storytelling opens the eyes of the audience and engages their emotions to discover the magic in their hearts. Using the imagination and mythical language, he connects you to the story of your life. He offers your Legend to help you write your own story and make your own ending.

You can find Jurri at his personal website www.loversdreamersandme.com.
Also, this book and many other stories are featured in Jurri's podcast. You can find it at www.legendsofthewind.com.

ABOUT THE ILLUSTRATOR

Alisha Schenck

As an artist, Alisha wants to explore different worlds and realms of the imagination and bring you there with her. She looks through windows and doors of creativity and creates access for everyone to enjoy. The things she sees are hidden, and she loves bringing them to light.

Her pieces are made with a variety of styles and mediums. She uses oils, acrylic, pen and ink, and digital media. All of these techniques come from her training as an alum of the ArtCenter College of Design in Pasadena, CA. May her paintings and artwork engage you and energize you to go on some amazing adventures.

Please check her shop from time to time as new pieces become available, either the original traditional paintings, select prints, or her original digital paintings. Thank you for letting us share her special worlds with you!

www.alishasimaginarium.com

SeraphCreative

Heaven's Heart for Earth

Seraph Creative is a collective of artists, writers, theologians & illustrators who desire to see the body of Christ grow into full maturity, walking in their inheritance as Sons Of God on the Earth.

Sign up to our newsletter to know about future exciting releases.

Visit our website:

www.seraphcreative.org

TESTIMONIALS

"Choosing the road less traveled by is often filled with moments of desperation. And I found myself desperate for encouragement and fuel as I questioned the path of my dreams and destiny. The dreams I believed that were placed in my heart were to the right, but I found myself taking a step to the left. And I landed back in my hometown, a literal and metaphorical desert.

A year or so into that journey, on my birthday, Jurri surprised me with a story — my story, "Rain of Heaven". And just like its title, this story washed over me and refreshed me with vision, hope, and encouragement.

This story, "Rain of Heaven", which was tailor made just for me, touched the deepest places of my heart and brought a new level of understanding and wisdom to the journey that I was currently walking out.

There's something about having a tangible story written about you. It brings a sense of significance and validation not only to your identity but your journey. Jurri not only writes an imaginative story full of fascinating characters and settings, but he adds depth to these stories with specific insight woven into the story, tailored made for the individual person. The story is inspired by "Rain of Heaven," which continues to move me. It's not just a fairytale, it functions as a mirror as well. I can't help but weep at how every detail of our lives becomes beautifully woven together to tell a unique story. A story that's worth being written about and shared — Shared, in order to encourage the next person on their unique life journey."

— Patrice Patrick

TESTIMONIALS cont.

"I was so excited to receive Jurri's story about me as a birthday gift last year. It was a delightful and fun encouragement then, and as I read it now, a year later, I am amazed again at how it still applies to my life and encourages me on my life journey. It contained insights that really affirm who I am and gives me the courage to keep pursuing my dreams. His stories are amazing!

What an enduring treasure for anyone who has the opportunity to have one written for them. You won't want to miss the secrets revealed in yours!"

— Phoebe

"I wanted more! I wanted more stories about me, and that's the truth. And my two stories are so vastly different and they both edify really different parts about me, which is really incredible. So know, these stories don't even have a repeated idea in them, even if there's some bleed over. I would say they both can give edification to my ability to interact with people. And so if one story can touch your heart? I mean truly, this man is gifted to write a story that really frees us up from the kind of distractions and lies and junk that tried to get us not to be who we are.

Well, the world tries to tell us, well, we're not that good at all or maybe I shouldn't be talking to people because I'm dying from my illness and what advice do I have? I haven't lived enough life. I really hadn't. I haven't done much more than really try and survive the physical stuff that's been in my life. Well, I'm on the other side of that now, so this story still helps and edifies: this is who I am and even though all of the health stuff is behind me, this is something that I can take with me as I move forward."

— Barbara Dumont

TESTIMONIALS cont.

"In a world where we've lost the art of storytelling, Jurri Schenck gives the gift of words by painting a picture and giving glimpses into the deep places of your heart. He writes these stories where he has no idea about the subject ahead of time, and he gives it to you. My story from Jurri has just changed my life.

I actually got a story from Jurri on my 25th birthday and he wrote this beautiful story about deep things, deep passions, dreams of mine that I had and he told it in this beautiful way that these words painted this beautiful picture.

And really, in this world, in this age right now, we have many things at our fingertips; we have video; we have things that just are where words are meaningless and easy to read. But to have a personalized story that changes your life, that reminds you of who you are and that when the times get really tough, you re-read that story out loud and it repaints a picture of the dreams of your heart, that's worth it!

And for me, it was a gift. Anyone who has a chance of getting this story it's going to be a gift and I guarantee it's going to change your life. I am so grateful that that was my gift on my 25th birthday. I recommend it. And I can't speak any higher of his stories."

— Melissa Otis

TESTIMONIALS cont.

"Legends of the Wind is incredibly important because I think myth is important, I think story is important. This is the way the power of a story can change the life of someone. It can help someone see a perspective that's just a little bit different from their own, and it might help them see a situation or an issue or a problem that's a little bit different from the way they see it. So, all of a sudden they can find an answer that's different from what they would have come to without that myth or that story.

Myths period, story period is so important to people's lives so they can kind of follow a track, so they can see how good it can be. They can also be warned of how bad it can be. But how good is it when you know they can finally see? How good it is when you can have something to reach for, whether that's reaching within something good inside of them, that they get from the story or reaching for something on the outside of a career or something on the outside, that they can aspire to.

I think the story is what drives all of us. I don't think we have really much of anything without a story. I think it's very important. So, please guys, it's so powerful to have your own story written about you, to have that power in your life. The story is kind of telling you about your life before you know it. Jurri and Alisha are super gifted. They really, really have a gift for this. So, get your story written. Get your story written and see what's on Father's heart for you guys. The myth is out there that you can relate to. I think it's going to be really fun, and I think it's going to help you a lot."

— Niles Rivers

BECOME A LEGEND

Do you want to become a Legend and receive your own story? Do you want to discover your identity and destiny through a personal myth, fairytale, or parable?

**Sign up and join our
mailing list for future updates.
www.legendsofthewind.com**